Hello? Anyone there?"

Her heart pounding, Valentine closed her eyes and willed the man to go away. Just a little while longer and she would get out of this mess.

Raleigh opened the door wider. To his surprise, he was greeted by the sight of Valentine with her leg perched on a chair, her skirt panels dragging on the floor as they parted over a slim, shapely thigh.

"Excuse me," he said, causing Valentine to open her blue eyes wide in chagrin at the man who had stared at her.

"You're not supposed to be back here!" Valentine insisted. "Please leave."

"Whoa!" he said in a teasing voice, holding out his hands. "I just want to know who you are."

"That's not really any of your business."

"I beg to differ," he said calmly. "I think it is some of my business. My name is Raleigh Coseegan, and I'm paying for your performance tonight..."

Megan Lane

Megan Lane is the author of twenty-eight short stories and more than thirty romance novels written under various pseudonyms. The two brightest moments in her writing career were selling the first romance book she wrote and the first psychological suspense.

She has taught writing classes, appeared on many television shows, and spoken all over the country. A veteran traveler, she has visited forty-six states, the South Pacific, twelve European countries, Mexico, the Caribbean and Bahama Islands, and China.

She is a member of the Authors' Guild, Romance Writers of America, Virginia Romance Writers, Mystery Writers of America Inc., and the Carolina Crime Writers' Association.

Her hobbies include movies, live theater, concerts, and, of course, reading.

MEGAN LANE
NO TURNING BACK

BERKLEY BOOKS, NEW YORK

NO TURNING BACK

First edition published September 1989

ISBN: 0-425-11752-9

"Second Chance at Love" and the butterfly emblem are trademarks belonging to Jove Publications, Inc. The name "BERKLEY" and the "B" logo are trademarks belonging to Berkley Publishing Corporation.

Second Chance at Love books are published by
The Berkley Publishing Group
200 Madison Avenue, New York, NY 10016

Printed in the United States of America

10 9 8 7 6 5 4 3 2 1

NO TURNING BACK

CHAPTER ONE

VALENTINE SMITH DREW in a deep breath and told herself that she was in the midst of a very silly, totally foolish dream. This wasn't *really* happening to her. She wasn't *actually* standing behind a stage curtain dressed in an oversized bra decorated with baubles, bangles, and beads.

She *didn't* have on what amounted to no more than a coin belt and several pieces of sheer fabric slung low on her hips—*very low*, because the hip band was too large. Not her. Not the woman who was struggling so hard to make a go of her bakery shop in a small Virginia town where shops were so entrenched that they were passed down from generation to generation, reputation included.

She sighed wearily. She didn't want her reputation even slightly smudged. After her fiancé, Brady, had

1

embezzled money from the bank where they both worked in Boston, then made it look as though she had done it, Valentine had been devastated. She had thought Brady was in love with her; it had been crushing to discover he was only using her.

Fortunately, the bank president had trusted her. Evidence had proven conclusively that Valentine had had nothing to do with the crime, but it had frightened her forever of scandal.

And maybe even love. She liked to think that wasn't the case. She still had dreams, but she was going to be very, very careful when it came to giving her heart away a second time.

"Hurry up, Val!"

The sound of her name on Tricia Haldran's lips convinced her that this was no dream. She *was* really here, about to commit social suicide.

"The music's going to start in a few minutes!" Tricia added urgently. "They sound like wild men out there. They might tear the place apart if we keep them waiting."

"They might tear the place apart if I come out." Valentine groaned and shook her head. "I'm sorry, Tricia. I just don't think I can do it. I don't know why on earth I let you and Pat talk me into this. I'm not a belly dancer, for crying out loud!"

"Let me remind you why," the taller woman said, her exasperated look telling Valentine in no uncertain terms that there was little time left for procrastinating. "Money and friendship, in that order. You need the money and Pat needed someone to fill in for her."

"Oh. Those were the reasons," Valentine said, having completely forgotten them in her panic.

Pat had caught the flu and couldn't make it. But worse—much worse—was the fact that Mr. Carruthers had raised the shop's rent by fifty dollars, leaving Valentine financially strapped. At the moment, however, she was little convinced that even those reasons justified such a foolish act.

"If you'd been nice to Mr. Carruthers, you wouldn't have money worries," Tricia said sweetly, as though reading Valentine's mind. "Honey, he wants to be your sugar daddy. All you had to do was smile and share a few dinners with him. He would have been perfectly happy and you would have been better off."

"Shame on you, Tricia!" Valentine said. "I don't want a sugar daddy. That silly man is old enough to be my grandfather."

Tricia laughed. "You're out of step with the times, Val. Mr. Carruthers is probably pushing sixty, you're twenty-five—December-May liaisons are very fashionable these days."

"I don't care how fashionable they are! I don't want any part of one, and I won't be coerced into one!" Valentine retorted indignantly. "I can't even imagine that old fool thinking he could use money to make me go out with him!"

Darn it all, she told herself. It was her bad luck that Mr. Carruthers had discovered that she was not only relatively new in town, but all alone. She had made the mistake of thinking he was trying to be kind to her when he had shown such a personal interest.

"Well, just remember the steps we practiced and you'll be fine," Tricia said, her voice only slightly soothing as she adjusted her own exotic costume a final time. "After all, you did take the belly-dancing class."

"Yes, *weeks* ago," Valentine said, glancing at the other woman's abundant bosom and tanned, defined abdomen.

She scrutinized her own pale, slim figure, which looked pathetic in Pat's costume. "And I never mastered belly dancing. I'm just not equipped for slithering and wiggling and making sinuous movements. My snake movement looks like someone stepped on it and tried to kill it, and my camel walk looks like my camel died of thirst in the desert."

She shook her head emphatically. "I just can't belly dance. I only took the class for fun, and to meet people. I never intended to dance in public!"

"Val," Tricia said, "you're much too obsessed with your image. You're making too much of this. You'll do fine. You're used to dealing with the public, serving up all those outrageously fattening goodies and making little jokes. Look at this as a night's fun and enjoy it."

"Enjoy it?" Valentine repeated in disbelief. "This isn't the same as meeting people in the shop. *I* feel like a piece of pastry. In fact, I feel like a—a tart!"

When her friend laughed again, shaking her head, Valentine reminded herself that Tricia and Pat did this not only to help finance their new dance studio, but also because they *wanted* to. Dance was their life.

"You know it's different for you and Pat," Val added hastily, not meaning to offend. "Why, just look at me," she said plaintively. "I look perfectly awful. I bake rolls for this restaurant. If someone here should recognize me, I don't know what I'd do. I was insane to agree to this. This is the kind of thing people talk about forever."

"You're really exaggerating this," Tricia said. "Anyway, it's too late now," the dark woman said with a sigh. "We were desperate and you agreed. I'm afraid you're committed. Put your veil on and let's get out there."

Valentine groaned again. "I'm not kidding. You'd be better off to go it alone. I'll only embarrass both of us."

"Listen," Tricia said, "the uncle paid for two dancers—" She paused and rolled her eyes. "Oh, what an uncle!"

Valentine wasn't sure what that meant and before she could ask, Tricia continued. "Anyway, he's going to get two. You promised, and we both need the money. The prospective bridegroom really wanted a harem of dancing girls, a send-off into marriage that he and his buddies would never forget, but there just weren't any more dancers available. Now quit complaining and get a smile on your face. You look like somebody's holding a gun to your head."

"I feel like it," Valentine said ruefully. Obviously Tricia didn't know what it was to be humiliated.

Yet she knew Tricia was right, and she didn't see how she could let the other woman down. Loyalty was high on her list of required character traits. She had given her word.

Dance! She had never been a dancer, not even by the most generous definition of the word. She didn't have a good sense of rhythm. She was always one of those people who stepped on her partner's toes and made embarrassed jokes about having two left feet.

She was a baker in a small shop in a conservative

part of the town, and happy to be pursuing her dream: to follow in her grandfather's footsteps and have a bakery of her own.

Her fondest memories were of the times she had spent in her grandfather's shop. She had found, though, that she could earn considerably more money working in a bank after high school graduation than becoming an apprentice in a bakery. She gradually worked her way up, eventually taking a comfortable position in a bank in Boston. Having attained so much yet still finding herself restless and unfulfilled had forced Val to take a hard look at her life and her options. She had made up her mind to chase that early dream until she caught it, and had moved to this small southern town.

She sighed. This had certainly never been part of her dream. She was about to dance in an outrageous costume in front of a bunch of men.

"It's just first-time stage fright," Tricia insisted. "You'll be all right once you get out there. Besides, there's no turning back now."

"Unfortunately," Valentine whispered, glancing at herself in the mirror.

She gazed down at the bra covered with satin, spangles, coins, and tassels. The creamy beads that were suspended from the center of the tilted cups had more color than her skin. And no matter how strategically designed the cups were, they didn't give *her* the illusion of voluptuousness. She was a sad specimen.

Glancing lower, she cringed at the sight of the hip band riding very low across her abdomen; it, too, was decorated with an assortment of things that jingled, jangled, and jiggled. Graduated lengths of chains with more coins were draped so that they were longer in front and shorter on the sides and back.

Under the hip band were tights and panty hose rolled down below her tummy so they wouldn't be obvious. Over the hip band were the filmy pink chiffon panels of her costume. The skirt was designed to permit total freedom for leg movements. A second skirt of sheer panels was tied over the first so that it could easily be removed as she danced.

A quick look at her ankles revealed more jewelry, even a *toe* ring, she thought in distaste. "Val, stop acting like you're committing a sin!"

Valentine whirled around at Tricia's cry of impatience, and every part of her seemed to make a noise.

"Now remember what I told you. If you can't follow me, just improvise. You'll be fine." With a wink, Tricia tucked the ends of her veil into her bra and waited for the music.

Doing the same with her veil, Valentine drew a shuddering breath. Her insides were quivering so severely that she was sure she could never make it out on the stage of the private back room of the restaurant. She'd been told that this was an early bachelor party, arranged at this time to accommodate the most friends. A bachelor party! And she and Tricia were the entertainment!

A final glance in the mirror revealed a dark stranger with black brows and black lashes and even a black mole. Thanks heavens for the disguise!

With one last nervous pat, she made sure her dark wig was in place over her long blond hair. Hoping against hope that the prospective bridegroom had only a handful of friends, she braced herself to move with Tricia through the part in the velvet curtain.

Suddenly the exotic Middle-Eastern music started and Tricia picked up the exhilarating beat, moving easily out on the stage to the sound of shouts and applause. In her wake, acutely aware of how tantalizingly and enticingly Tricia moved beneath the sheer covering of the veil, Valentine tried to find the right rhythm. She decided she didn't have to worry about shimmying and shaking; she was so nervous, she was doing it automatically!

After just a teaser of a dance, Tricia stepped up to the microphone. "Good evening," she said exuberantly while Valentine quaked at her side, gooseflesh on her arms despite the warmth of the room. "I'm Farrah and this is—Angelina."

Valentine glanced sideways at the other woman. They hadn't discussed names, but it really didn't matter. Angelina was as good as anything.

"We're here to entertain," Tricia continued. "It's our fondest hope that we'll make this evening memorable for you!"

There was more shouting and clapping. Wolf whistles and hoots filled the room. Valentine somehow gathered the nerve to look out over the crowd of men. Surely she was hyperventilating; she felt dizzy. She had to keep telling herself that she was not going to faint.

She also told herself that no one man should have that many friends; there were thirty or forty of them.

Her eyes settled on the restaurant owner, and realized from Tricia's description that it was *his* son who was getting married! Great, there goes his business. She shifted her gaze to another man sitting at the table. He didn't seem to fit in well with the rest of the group. She didn't recall seeing him around town, but then she had only been here for six months. Though the town was small by almost any standards, it wasn't small enough that she'd ever know everyone.

He was gorgeous, looking suave and sophisticated with his curly dark blond hair and dark eyes. Dark eyes that were staring directly into hers, she realized with shock. She was sure she sensed disapproval in his steady gaze. His eyes lingered only a moment before he abruptly looked away and leaned toward the groom in a conspiratorial whisper.

Raleigh Coseegan felt like a relic, a dinosaur, ancient and fossilized here in the midst of his nephew's bachelor party. Several of the young men were in their twenties and already had families of their own. They were having a ball; he had never heard so much laughter and good-natured teasing, and he thought he had heard everything.

He envied them their ability to savor such an evening. At thirty-six, he could hardly get excited about amateur belly dancers. He had done too much, seen too much, become too world-weary. He shifted in his seat.

Not that he was oblivious to the sensuous beauty of the dance or the beauty of lovely young women, he reminded himself. In his travels, he had seen belly dancing performed in the Middle East by women who had learned the movements when they were little girls and had perfected them to an art form.

But these two women— His practiced gaze slid over

them. The taller, fuller-figured dancer was the one he'd spoken to at the studio. Her movements were more than competent, but the smaller one—well, she was something else. He was hard put to find a term.

He was in for an evening with a pair who had probably taken a dance class at the local Y, he thought, smiling. Belly dancers were what his nephew, Randolph, wanted, and Raleigh hadn't found a surplus from which to choose. He turned his smile to Randolph, then glanced back at the smaller of the two dancers, Angelina.

In truth, she hardly looked as if she could keep her costume on, let alone dance in it. Her movements were —um—enthralling. He settled back into his chair, noting, with admiration, that Angelina had guts if not talent. This could very well prove to be entertaining, after all.

Frantically observing the gorgeous man's smile, Valentine mustered a semblance of one herself. She took a tiny bit of comfort in his unexpected friendliness. Maybe she would get through this evening after all. Maybe.

She didn't even hear what Tricia was saying. When the music began again, it was as if she had been put on automatic pilot. Abruptly, she began to dance, or at least to try. Following Tricia's lead, she imitated her friend's movements, swirling the sheer pink veil around her body, swaying and spinning with the floating rhythm of the colored cloth.

She knew the idea was to create a graceful, ethereal illusion with the veil. While she wasn't foolish enough to think she had accomplished that, she did manage to get through most of the song with more finesse than she had anticipated. That is, right until the end.

Completing the veil movements, Valentine clasped the garment in one hand, brought it up over her head, twirled it once, then twice, then a third time before flinging it dramatically to the floor.

Unfortunately, she didn't quite master the maneuver. As she cast the veil aside, the filmy material caught her curly wig, dragging it off.

Reaching desperately for the black locks, Valentine blindly righted them as rapidly as she could. But not before strands of brilliant blond hair glistened under the stage lights. Some of them still peeked out from beneath the harsh wig after Valentine had adjusted the phony hair, looking like spun gold against dark velvet.

Grateful not to have lost the wig altogether, she forced a nervous smile to her lips and turned her back to the audience as Tricia did, in preparation for the next dance. She thought she heard a few chuckles and suspected they were directed at her. She knew if she thought about it, she wouldn't be able to continue. Her face flaming, Valentine used the moment to summon enough courage to turn back around.

Raleigh didn't miss the chuckles from the audience either, and he found a smile forming on his own lips. He had been delighted to see the golden hair exposed beneath the black. He had also caught a glimpse of sky-blue eyes beneath the sooty black lashes. The name *Angelina* just might suit the woman after all. Beneath the garish disguise, there just might be an angel, ivory-skinned, golden-haired, and youthful.

How he would love to find such a refreshing crea-
ture. He had come here three days ago to attend his
nephew's upcoming wedding. The visit was providing a
much needed break. This was only the third time he'd
been here since he had helped his sister and her family
move here seven years ago.

He shook his head, recalling how surprised he had
been when Carolyn told him that she, Tod, and the children were moving from California to open up a restaurant. They wanted to get away from the rat race, she had
explained, and this would be a good place for the children.

Although he had helped them choose the restaurant,
and even invested a considerable sum of money, Raleigh
had only stayed a day. The small town had made him
feel claustrophobic. He had come for Christmas, loaded
with presents, but he hadn't visited for very long.
Always restless, Raleigh had found himself leaving just
two days after he'd arrived. His car, he recalled had
been approximately thirty presents lighter on the trip
home. He had left a family happily gathered around the
fireplace.

As heartwarming a picture as they had made, it was
not the life for him. Always a maverick, Raleigh had
deliberately chosen a solitary path, one laden with ad-
venture, danger and challenge. Though he always
sought, and found, respite in his visits with the family,
the need to move on was always there.

He drew in a steadying breath. Oddly, during this
stay in Virginia, he had surprised himself by liking the
town, by seeing what his brother-in-law meant about the

peaceful setting and friendly people. The narrow streets, sheltered by ancient trees laden with leaves the fresh green of spring, were a welcome distraction from the heat and barren deserts of the Middle East.

It seemed miraculous to walk down a street without worrying about bombs and snipers. Here people still took evening strolls and sat on their front porches talking about how their gardens were growing.

This was an oasis, he realized. He had forgotten how important it was to take time to smell the flowers—literally. He was ready to sit and let the world stop for a while.

More and more, he was finding that his career as an overseas journalist had lost much of its appeal in these days of terrorism and tragedy. Constantly writing about misery was taking its toll. Maybe so many years of living on the edge had finally gotten to him. Recently he had discovered that he much preferred to write his travel books and manage his considerable investments. He was even thinking about trying his hand at fiction.

Glancing down at his drink, he idly stirred it. As he had become involved in the upcoming wedding, he had realized just how much he enjoyed his relationship with Tod, Carolyn, his ten-year-old niece, Tina, and Randolph. He felt as though he belonged somewhere for a change.

He frowned as the memory of that last Christmas here surged into his mind. Wasn't that why he had rushed off in such a hurry? Hadn't the domestic scene tugged at his heartstrings until he had frightened himself with his thoughts? Abruptly, he remembered what had disturbed him most of all—the realization of how lonely he was.

"Uncle Raleigh?"

"Hmm?" he murmured distractedly, giving his attention to his nephew.

"Is the one with the black hair for real?"

Raleigh looked back up at the stage just in time to see Angelina trip on one of the side panels of her skirt as she attempted to negotiate a hip-rolling motion while moving in a large open circle. The hip band holding up her skirt shifted precariously low on one side while the woman tried futilely to catch her balance with some semblance of poise. She managed to stay upright, but the attempt was a riot.

She moved forward, then sideways, then abruptly crashed into the other dancer, who was apparently trying to come to her aid. The other woman was momentarily caught off-balance, but she quickly regained her equilibrium.

Shaking his head in disbelief, Raleigh could only try not to break into laughter along with the rest of the audience. The woman couldn't have been more amusing if she were part of a professional comedy act.

He hadn't hired a comedy act, but then he hadn't hired the woman with the black hair, he suddenly realized. Both of the women he had hired had been taller and more full-figured than Angelina.

"Have you ever seen such craziness in your life, Raleigh?" Tod asked, leaning nearer to be heard over the laughter. "That Angelina is a hoot! I didn't know you'd gotten a comedy duo. Maybe I should book this act on weekends instead of the band. I've never thought of belly dancers because this town is so conservative, but I bet women would laugh at this act as much as men."

Valentine tried her best to free her feet from the tangle of chiffon panels after she stepped on one, but when she moved backward, she succeeded only in putting herself in more jeopardy. The entire hip band had shifted to her left side and it took every ounce of her concentration to stay upright and still appear to be dancing.

Her face was flaming as she fought the tangle of pink under her feet. Alas, she realized she had no choice but to adjust the hip band before she could walk, let alone dance. With a desperate glance at Tricia, she did just that, tugging the band back into place over her panty hose.

This time the audience howled openly with laughter. She was so inept and ridiculous that she was hilarious. Even Tricia was smiling when Valentine looked woefully at her.

If Valentine could have died right there and sunk into the floor forever, she would have been eternally grateful; unfortunately, that wasn't to be her fate.

Suddenly the men were pounding their fists on the table and shouting "More! More!" as if they thought she had planned to make an absolute imbecile of herself. To her added shame, she looked right into the face of the one observer she had thought sympathetic to her plight; he, too, was laughing.

*   *   *

Raleigh had lost the battle to remain unmoved by the dance. The woman was entertaining him as he hadn't been entertained in far too long. He had forgotten how truly wonderful it was to laugh with abandon, to totally seize the pleasure of the moment. He had needed this time. Angelina was delightful, a natural comic in an obviously well-rehearsed act. She was the funniest thing he had seen in years.

He admired her ability to get up there on the stage and entertain an audience. Who could she be? he wondered.

Before Valentine could turn around and run for her life, Tricia appeared at her side, looping arms with her. Practically dragging the younger woman, Tricia somehow got them both up to the microphone.

"There'll be more," she announced with a huge smile. "Just keep your places while we take a short break; we'll be back!"

The compelling beat of the music continued while Tricia guided Valentine back through the part in the curtain. Valentine didn't care *how* she got off the stage— only that she did. She would have settled for the old vaudeville hook if it would have helped her escape.

CHAPTER TWO

TRICIA TOUCHED VALENTINE'S shoulder. "Boy, did you make a mess of things, but what a hit you became!" she practically crowed. "They loved it. I don't know how you managed to make so many blunders in a row, but I do know I've never had such audience response!"

Valentine shook her head. "I don't know how either, believe me. I was trying to do it right."

Tricia laughed. "You did do it right—whatever *it* was. When we go back out there, you just keep right on doing it."

Valentine was aghast. "You can't be serious! I wouldn't go back out there for a million dollars! I've never been so humiliated in my life!"

Well, almost never, she silently added to herself. This humiliation was different from being called a criminal. Being a fool wasn't quite as bad, but it bore its

17

own ugly stigma for a woman who wanted a spotless reputation.

"I wanted to sink right through the floor and die!" she added, glancing down. "This costume is partly to blame. It's so big that it's in my way. I didn't dance this badly in class or during the practice session with you."

"Don't complain. The audience thinks it was all part of the act, and they loved it!" Tricia declared triumphantly. "And you *were* funny. If only you could have seen yourself! I declare it was all *I* could do to keep from laughing."

"We weren't out there to do a comedy routine," Valentine reminded her.

"Nonsense! We were there to entertain by belly dancing—whatever form that took."

"I don't believe this!" Valentine cried. "I will never live this down, and you're acting like we planned the entire thing!"

"Calm down," Tricia coaxed. "Don't you know that this is how great acts are established? Quite unintentionally? Fate has handed me this, and I mean to play it to the hilt."

"Tricia," Valentine said solemnly, "I'm a baker, caught up in this degrading moment only for tonight. Don't talk as if we're about to become the act of the century. I wouldn't do this again if my life depended on it!"

"We'll see," Tricia said pensively, clearly trying to humor the younger woman. "But now that it's happened, why not make the best of it? Why not roll with it? I truly believe the men don't know we didn't plan it this way. We have another half hour to work. Now tell me what's better—being the joke of the night, or *making* the joke of the night?"

Valentine sighed wearily. Of course it was better to make the joke, but could she go out there again? She didn't think she could; not only that, she wasn't willing to try.

"I've been mortified enough to last a lifetime," she said. "You go out and dance alone. The men deserve that, at least. After all, what were you telling me before we went on about legitimacy and art of the dance?"

The laughter and confusion of Valentine's fiasco momentarily fading, Tricia became thoughtful. "You're probably right," she said at last. "I just got so caught up in their reaction. Besides, we didn't promise them two dancers for the entire evening. However, I did promise that *we* would return," she added.

She snapped her fingers. "I know! Later you can come out just one more time to dance with the zills."

"I can't use the zills," Valentine wailed despairingly. "I can't keep up with the music, this costume, or myself, let alone try to use finger cymbals. It'll just be another disaster if I try."

"*I* think so," Tricia said with a satisfied grin. "I'm almost positive it's a sure way to leave them laughing."

Feeling dejected, Valentine agreed. "I'm sure you're right about leaving them laughing."

"Then you'll do it—just one more dance?"

"No!" Valentine countered. "I'd rather walk into the lion's den."

"You might do that too, if you don't go back out there like we promised the uncle who hired us," Tricia said. "Somehow I don't think he's a man to accept less than what was agreed upon. Come on. Just one more dance and we'll quit."

Valentine sighed and nodded. "Just one more moment of total degradation."

"You'll live through it," Tricia assured her with a big smile. "And someday you'll even laugh about it. After all, how much can it hurt?"

Valentine found herself thinking that Tricia had never experienced such humiliation or she wouldn't have to ask; before she could say anything, Tricia spoke again.

"I'll come for you when I'm ready for you to dance." Then she rushed off before Valentine could comment.

Raleigh watched the woman called Farrah as she danced several more dances. Clearly the straight half of the twosome, she was quite good. But it was the other dancer he was interested in. He wanted to know who she was. His curiosity about the blonde was only enhanced by her absence.

"As much as I hate to go, I'd better see how the rest of business is doing," Tod said, interrupting Raleigh's thoughts. "I'll be back in a few minutes."

Raleigh nodded, then decided to take the opportunity to talk to the blonde before she came back out on stage. "Excuse me," he said to Randolph and the table in general. He smiled wryly when he saw that they were too engrossed in Farrah to take much notice of his departure.

Raleigh was familiar with the building, which had once been a never-quite-successful nightclub before Tod turned it into a restaurant. Tod had cleverly sound-proofed and partitioned off the two back rooms where the stage was and offered entertainment on occasion, or private meeting rooms, depending upon the town's needs.

Raleigh went down the hall and knocked twice on the door of the cubicle that served as a dressing area. There was no sound other than the dramatic beat of Middle Eastern music.

Standing with one leg braced on a wooden chair while she tried to readjust her nylons and costume, Valentine cringed when she heard the knock. Who had come backstage, and why? She certainly didn't want to see anyone. She was going to do her last bit and go home. She didn't want anybody ever to find out who she was.

Raleigh rapped again; when he didn't hear a response, he opened the door the tiniest bit and called out, "Hello. Anyone there?"

Her heart pounding, Valentine closed her eyes and willed the man to go away. Just a little while longer and she would get out of this mess . . .

Raleigh opened the door wider. To his surprise, he was greeted by the sight of Angelina with her leg perched on a chair, her skirt panels dragging on the floor as they parted over a slim, shapely thigh.

"Excuse me," he said, causing Valentine to open her blue eyes wide in chagrin when she saw that it was the man who had stared at her. "I . . . well, no one answered."

She felt like sinking inside herself as she met his amused gaze. Oh, why did it have to be him, of all people?

She quickly put her foot down. "And no one said you could come in," she shot back.

He shrugged and smiled. "I missed you on stage. I wanted to meet you."

"You're not supposed to be back here!" Valentine insisted. "Please leave."

Raleigh was surprised by her obvious nervousness. He didn't see any reason for her to be so anxious.

"Whoa!" he said in a teasing voice, holding out his hands as if to ward off blows. "I just want to know who you are."

"That's not really any of your business." What a nightmare come true; the *last* thing she wanted was someone knowing who she was. "Now please leave before I call—before I call somebody."

She had really aroused his curiousity, and Raleigh smiled faintly. Something wasn't right here. Why was this beautiful mystery so hostile? Even if she didn't think he should be in her dressing room, wasn't she overreacting just a tad? The inquisitive reporter in him had been awakened. He wanted some answers.

"I beg to differ," he said calmly. "I think it is some of my business. My name is Raleigh Coseegan, and I'm paying for your performance tonight."

Her eyes widening, Valentine looked anxiously at the door. So this was the uncle who had hired Tricia and Pat. Now she knew why Tricia had rolled her eyes.

"I'd just like to know who you are," Raleigh repeated, unable to understand why she was making such a fuss. "And what the story is on your dance routine."

Embarrassed, Valentine lowered her blue eyes. He had seen through her, despite Tricia's contention that no one would know whether the awful gaffes were intentional. She couldn't stand here and tell him she was a dancer, could she? Not only was it a lie, *he* knew it was a lie. She could feel her face turning redder by the moment.

"Will you please talk to me?" Raleigh murmured, sensing her discomfort and truly not wanting to make her unhappy.

A new rush of color filled Valentine's cheeks. She'd known she could never get away with this. She'd warned Tricia not to think she could. And what now? What was she going to say to this man who so obviously felt cheated?

She met his eyes, suddenly overcome with a desire at least to explain what had happened. Their gazes held; she was so mesmerized for a moment that she couldn't think of what to say.

Suddenly Tricia burst into the room. Valentine had never been so glad to see anyone in her life. She'd been about to do something very foolish, and she wasn't even sure what. Val instinctively stepped away from Raleigh, relief rushing through her.

"Come on!" Tricia cried breathlessly. "It's time for the final number."

She came to a dead stop when she saw Raleigh, but hesitated only briefly before recovering admirably and flashing him a big, professional smile.

"I hope you're enjoying the show," she said smoothly, grabbing the zills. "Will you excuse us please? We've got to run."

She thrust a pair of zills into Valentine's hand and pulled her along. With mixed emotions, Valentine followed. She hadn't really wanted to admit to this gorgeous stranger that he had been tricked, and while she didn't want to go back on stage, it was definitely the lesser of two evils.

When she stopped behind the velvet curtain, her heart was pounding. She glanced back over her shoulder to see if the man had followed. Her heart beat faster when she saw Raleigh Coseegan standing there. This time she was grateful to vanish through the parted curtain after Tricia.

Raleigh had calmly strolled behind the two women, and now he watched as they disappeared through the part in the curtain. What was all the secrecy about? Why all the intrigue? They certainly hadn't wanted to deal with him. That only interested him more. He smiled at their naiveté.

He was not a man easily shaken off, a trait that had come in quite handy throughout his career. Blessed with the patience of a saint, the nose of a bloodhound, and—until his last scrape with death—nerves of steel, he was neither discouraged nor dismayed by the most artful evasive tactics. It had taken him no time at all to assess the efforts of the dynamic duo as strictly amateur, but charming nonetheless. These ladies had tried to run a game on him but he had been too entertained to be angry. Now was the time for truth. After all, wasn't he entitled to an explanation?

Shaking his head in amusement, he went to the side of the curtain, pulled it back a little, and watched as the two women began another dance.

If it was possible—and he wasn't sure it was—Angelina was even more amusing than she had been before. He actually laughed aloud as she tried to get her feet, hips, head, and zills in motion simultaneously only to lose the rhythm entirely.

Valentine heard his laughter and quickly glanced over her shoulder. She wished she could stop right in the middle of the dance and . . . and punch him in the face!

Yet she knew her anger was misplaced. After all, she was the one making a laughingstock of herself. She couldn't call what she was doing dancing. How could she blame him for laughing?

She looked away. She knew what was really bothering her. As ridiculous as it was, she found the man extremely attractive even though he was having such a grand time at her expense. Business, Valentine. You have to concentrate on business. Now is *not* the time to let a man fill your thoughts, no matter how attractive he is.

Had she so soon forgotten what Brady had done to her? She was going to be exceptionally careful before she led with her heart instead of her head a second time.

After what seemed to be an eternity, the music finally ended. The laughter, however, continued unabated. Clasping Valentine's hand in hers, Tricia went over to the microphone.

"We've loved entertaining you," she gushed over the sound of the merriment. "I hope we've contributed to a successful evening. If any of you want to book us again, we're listed in the book under TP Entertainment."

The young revelers applauded and whistled. Some of them shouted their appreciation. To Tricia's delight and Valentine's dismay, they even gave the women a standing ovation.

Valentine remained on the stage only long enough to be polite; then she brushed past Raleigh so rapidly that he didn't have a chance to detain her.

"Farrah," he called as Tricia went past, "I need to talk to you."

"Gee, could you give us a few minutes?" Tricia asked politely.

Raleigh nodded. There was no rush. For some inexplicable reason, he felt he could wait for Angelina indefinitely. And he was mystified.

"Oh geez," Tricia moaned when she entered the dressing room, causing Valentine to look up anxiously. "Raleigh Coseegan wants to talk to me."

"Raleigh Coseegan?" Valentine repeated innocently.

"You know, the uncle."

"Oh," Valentine said, her voice flagging. So, Raleigh Coseegan really was the man who had hired them.

Tricia brushed at her long hair. "Everyone else loved the show. I hope he isn't going to ask for his money back."

"Don't worry," Valentine said dryly, "he laughed too much himself to demand his money back. He was entertained. He got his money's worth."

She would not think of how he had moved her when he looked so deeply into her eyes, she told herself firmly. She would only let herself remember how he had laughed at her.

Tricia frowned. "I hope so. Still, maybe you'd better slip away. I'll talk to him after you're gone."

"Good idea," Valentine said, reaching for the long raincoat and scarf she'd worn over her costume. She hadn't heard anything that sounded better all evening. No one had to tell her twice to leave. If she was lucky, she'd never see Raleigh Coseegan again.

"Here goes," she murmured, opening the door. "Talk to you later."

When she peered out, her breath caught in her throat. Leaning against the wall, his hands shoved casually in his pockets, Raleigh was patiently waiting as though he had all the time in the world.

Valentine was struck by how polished and confident he seemed. She abruptly recalled how her heartbeat had quickened when he came into the room. She knew deep inside that the reason hadn't been only because she was afraid he would find out she was a fraud. It had been something more. But she didn't want to recall that.

Quickly and quietly she closed the door. "Good grief," she muttered. "He's right outside. What do we do now?"

"Outside? Raleigh Coseegan? You're not serious!" Tricia cried.

"Oh, but I am. He's—"

Abruptly, they both stopped talking as they heard someone coming. Valentine opened the door the tiniest bit.

"Raleigh, I wondered where you'd gone," they heard Tod say. "I've been looking for you."

Raleigh laughed. "I'm waiting for the belly dancers."

Tod chuckled. "So am I. I'm going to see about booking them here, alternating weekends with the band."

Valentine quickly shut the door, feeling herself caught up in a deepening nightmare. "Oh, Lord," she groaned. "Why me? How do these things happen to me?"

"What?" Tricia asked.

"It's Tod Duncan. He wants to hire us on alternate weekends."

Tricia squealed and clapped her hands. "That's wonderful!"

"It's not wonderful," Val said sternly. "It's awful. I wish I could just die right here." Tears of mortification shimmered in her blue eyes.

Seeing them, Tricia walked over to the younger woman and put her arm around her shoulders. "Valentine, I don't understand you. What's the big deal? Why are you getting so upset? You said yourself that you needed money. It would just be a few hours on the weekend, and you're the comedy part of the duo. So what?"

"So what?" Val hissed. "So what? I'll tell you so what, Tricia. I moved to this town to escape the humiliation of being accused of embezzling money from the bank where I was working."

She shook her head at Tricia's shocked expression and quickly continued. "I had nothing at all to do with it, believe me. I was simply a fool, taken in by a man who said he loved me. I never want another soul to stare or point at me as long as I remain on this earth."

"Oh, Val," Tricia murmured sympathetically, "you should have told me."

Val tried to smile through welling tears. She'd thought she'd gotten over the worst of the pain. She'd lost herself in her cooking classes, and she drove herself relentlessly at the bakery, trying to forget that people in

Boston had thought where there was smoke, there was fire, regardless of her name being cleared.

"I didn't think I'd ever tell anybody," she murmured. "I just want to forget, and I don't want anyone *ever* whispering about me again."

Tricia hugged the smaller woman. "Of course you don't. Oh, honey, I'd have understood if you'd told me. I sure don't want to add to your anguish."

This time Val did smile. "How was I to know I'd go out there and be an absolute fool? Even I couldn't have predicted how bad I'd be."

Tricia smiled. "Ah, but Valentine, you were fantastic!" She held up her hands. "No, I'm not asking you to do it again. I understand your need for respect and privacy and I see you still carry wounds, but don't regret tonight. No one will ever know, and it was incredible."

Valentine laughed lightly. "Maybe for you, Tricia. I'm just glad it's over."

Tricia frowned. "It's not quite, but we're going to do our best to get you out of here." She pulled the door open the slightest bit.

Raleigh was still talking with Tod, and the women could hear bits of their conversation. Tod had obviously asked something about Angelina.

"I'm a man who takes my laughs where I find them," Raleigh replied.

Valentine quickly shut the door again, her temper instantly flaring. She wasn't going to be one of his laughs!

"What do you know about that man?" she demanded, whirling around to face Tricia.

"Which one?"

"Raleigh Coseegan."

"He's a big-time foreign correspondent. He's also wealthy. That's why he was willing to pay us so well. He just came into town for a few weeks for his nephew's wedding."

"And a few laughs," Valentine said tightly.

Wasn't it just like her to be attracted to him, of all men? She hadn't even looked at another man seriously since she came to town. She'd hoped she'd learned her lesson from Brady, and yet this stranger made her tremble with his mere presence.

One thing was certain—she didn't have to force herself to remember that she was just a laugh for him now. He'd made it all too plain. She'd been the only one to be stirred by the intense look that had passed between them. She shouldn't have any difficulty at all recalling that. Obviously it had meant nothing to him.

Suddenly there was a knock on the door, which caused both women to jump. To Tricia's surprise, Valentine swung the door open wide.

"Yes?"

"Ready to talk?" Raleigh asked.

Tricia answered before Valentine could. There was nothing else they could do. "Yes."

"That's my exit line." Valentine tried to push past Raleigh. She didn't want to be in his company another moment.

"Wait a minute," he said, reaching out for her arm.

Too aware of his body heat as she stood inches from her, she watched as his firm fingers closed over her wrist to stop her, causing her skin to burn.

She looked down at the hairs growing on the back of

his strong hand and felt her pulse race. Oh, God, she couldn't really be reacting so wildly to this man, could she? With all her might, she strengthened her will to resist her crazy reaction to his touch.

"I don't do the discussion part of the business," she said in a betrayingly weak voice that had been intended to sound firm. "Please let me go."

He smiled at her, his gaze boldly meeting hers as he slowly freed her. "I thought you were going to change. I'd hoped we might have a late snack here in the restaurant."

Why did that suggestion cause her heart to pound anew? Hadn't she just told herself she'd been all the fool she was going to be for one night? Every instinct told her to get away from this man as soon as she could.

"Sorry," she said, not looking at him. "I have to get up very early in the morning."

"How about dinner tomorrow night?" he asked, undeterred.

She shook her head. He wasn't going to give up easily. "I have to get up early *every* morning."

"You aren't the woman I originally booked, are you?" he asked unexpectedly.

Valentine's pulse began to race. Here it came, she told herself. He was going to lower the boom on them.

"Actually," Tricia began, flashing him her biggest smile, "Pat was ill tonight. Angelina agreed to fill in for her."

"Well," Raleigh said, "Pat's misfortune was my good luck. I loved your act. To tell you the truth, it was the funniest thing I've seen in a long, long time."

Valentine pasted a smile on her lips. She wondered

what he would say if she told him how she had gone out on that stage with her knees shaking and her heart hammering, and done her best to perform the dances the way they were supposed to be.

"I'm glad you were entertained," she said dryly. She had no intention of letting him think she had meant to do anything else.

"Entertained? I was in stitches. I laughed so hard that my stomach muscles got sore."

Valentine's blue eyes swept along his hard muscled form. She doubted that anything really made him sore. He appeared to be in better shape than any man she had ever seen.

"Who are you?" he asked.

"TP Entertainment is Tricia Haldran and Patricia Shamus," Tricia interjected quickly.

"I see," Raleigh said. "And who are you?" He met Valentine's eyes again.

She had to look away. He had such a compelling, burning gaze that she was sure he always learned everything he wanted to know sooner or later. In this case, she intended for it to be much, much later—like never!

"It doesn't matter," she said. "I'm not the management part of the business."

"Oh, but it does matter to me," he said, his dark gaze holding her blue one. "My brother-in-law, Tod Duncan, has asked me to see if you're available to dance here on alternate weekends."

Valentine lowered her eyes. He had an air about him that made her suspect he was aware of the easy way he stirred her senses. He was way out of her league and they both knew it. Oh, why was she reacting to him this way? The only emotion she wanted to feel toward him was anger!

"I'm sorry. I'm not available," she replied crisply, trying her best to muster some ire toward him.

Raleigh frowned. "Not available? You *are* a professional dancer, aren't you?"

"Of course," Tricia said quickly.

There was a lengthy pause before Raleigh nodded. "Then when will you be available?" he asked, looking directly at Valentine.

Darn him and his persistence, Valentine told herself. But then, what would one expect from such a man?

"Never!" she stated irrevocably. "I'm out of the dance business as of tonight."

He suddenly gave her a lazy smile. "Now why's that, I wonder?"

Valentine's gaze darted to Tricia. This bullheaded man was set on making them confess that he had been deceived.

The women's eyes locked for a moment. Then Tricia seemed to shrug slightly, giving Raleigh her best smile. "As I explained, Va—Angelina is only a fill-in dancer, Mr. Coseegan. She's informed me that she doesn't want to fill in again after tonight, so I'm afraid that's that. Anyway, it would hardly be fair to Pat for me to take another regular partner."

Raleigh seemed thoughtful. "Tod doesn't think straight belly dancing would draw a crowd here. He thinks the wives in town might be a little too conservative. However, the two of you are funny enough to entertain anyone."

Tricia glanced at the intractable expression on Valentine's face. "As I said, Mr. Coseegan, it's either Pat and me, or no one."

Raleigh had dealt with enough people to know that Angelina wasn't going to relent, regardless of his coaxing. Still, he wanted to know who this mystery woman was. Her elusiveness intrigued him.

"And you won't tell me who you are?" he persisted, looking at Valentine again.

"No," she said adamantly. "I'd appreciate it if you wouldn't ask again. You do understand 'no,' don't you?"

Raleigh was surprised by the heat he felt rising under his shirt collar. He wasn't used to being rejected so bluntly by any woman. He understood "no" perfectly clearly, and he could accept it, too, when he had to. He wasn't the kind of man to force himself on any woman. Still, he had to have his say in this matter, just because the women thought they'd pulled something over on him.

"Yes," he said with quiet deliberation. "I'm college educated. I understand 'no.'" He glanced from woman to woman. "And I'm no fool, either. I didn't get what I requested—what I paid for—but since what I received was actually better than what I'd expected, I'd say my money was well spent. Good night, ladies."

He turned and walked from the room. Only the sharp slam of the door told the women how irritated he really was.

Once outside, Raleigh ran his hands through his hair. "Well, ol' boy," he muttered aloud, "you win some and you lose some. It's all in the game."

But he didn't like losing. He didn't like it at all. His

steps brisk, he went in search of Tod to tell him he could forget this dancing duo.

Valentine sighed heavily when Raleigh had gone. "Boy, what a stubborn man," she noted. "I'm glad that's over."

"I'm not sure it is," Tricia said pensively. "He really wanted to know who you were."

"Well, he's old enough for his wants not to hurt him," Valentine said sharply. Yet, to be honest, she couldn't help wishing she'd met him under some other circumstances. "He'll be gone soon anyway," she said aloud to remind herself of how foolish the whole situation was.

"How do you know?" Tricia asked.

Valentine looked surprised. "*You* said he was only going to be here for his nephew's wedding."

"I did say that," Tricia conceded, "though I don't know how long he plans to stay. The wedding is only weeks from Saturday, as you know. I've heard that it's going to be a fabulous affair—but then, you know more about that than I do since you're making the cake."

Valentine gasped. "Oh, Lord, I had forgotten that in my embarrassment. Of course I'm doing the cake. In fact, I'm catering the entire wedding. It's the Domini-Duncan wedding! I'm so upset that I don't know what's going on!"

The belly dance had been bad enough! Now there was Raleigh Coseegan to deal with. Surely there was no way she could avoid seeing him as they prepared for the wedding. Oh, why did he have to come back to the dressing room? Why hadn't he let her get through the evening and go on with her life?

"I'm afraid you can't avoid the man forever," Tricia said, confirming Val's thoughts. "A man like him will have a big hand in the function, you can be sure."

"Oh, good grief!" Valentine groaned. "The restaurant is my biggest account and the wedding my biggest job since I've been here."

"What are you going to do?" Tricia asked, her brow furrowed.

Valentine bit down on her lower lip, then straightened her spine, ignoring the jingling sounds her movements made. "I'm going on about my business," she declared. "Fortunately, no one knows who I am"—she looked at her friend—"so unless *you* tell, or Pat does, no one will *ever* know."

Tricia held up her hand. "Girl Scout's honor, I won't tell, and I can promise Pat won't. I'll talk to her."

Valentine smiled, really smiled, for the first time that night. "Then I think everything will be all right. Good night, Tricia."

She peeked out the door, saw no one, and left by the back way. All she wanted to do was put this night—and that man—behind her and get on with her bakery business.

CHAPTER THREE

AFTER THE RESTAURANT had closed that evening, Raleigh, Carolyn, and Tod were sitting at one of the tables sipping Cokes. The entire family worked in the restaurant, as well as other hired help, but most of the help had gone home. Tod and Carolyn were taking a much needed break.

"So," Tod asked, "did Farrah and Angelina want to do their routine on alternate weekends for us?"

Raleigh frowned, remembering Angelina's response all too well. "In a word, no!" he returned succinctly.

"Good grief, Raleigh, what did you say to them to get such a blunt rejection?" Tod teased. "Is that the effect of being a writer, or do you Coseegans simply not know how to be tactful? Your sister often has that problem, too. It's gotten her into trouble more than once in this town."

"Tod—" Carolyn protested, glancing from him to Raleigh.

"Don't 'Tod' me," he joked. "You know it's true." He looked at Raleigh. "When we first moved here, a few of the fine upstanding women found out that Carolyn's family fought on the Union side in the Civil War, that she didn't go to church every Sunday, and that she wasn't a Democrat. She had a devil of a time making friends with some of them for a while."

Raleigh smiled. "You're kidding, aren't you?"

"I'm not," Tod insisted. "Even now she's still trying to join some 'elitist' organization, which she's been told has a waiting list five years long, *or* that she needs two dozen sponsors, or some such thing."

Looking at Carolyn, Raleigh asked, "*Is* he kidding?"

Tod shook his head. "I'm telling the truth, Raleigh. You just don't know these places. You're a world traveler. This town *is* the world for most of these people. You don't ever dare say anything derogatory about anybody, for fear his aunt's cousin's great-uncle's brother is sitting right behind you. Why, half the town would stop patronizing the restaurant!"

Raleigh burst into laughter. "You're putting me on," he insisted.

"Well, yes, a little," Tod admitted. "But not entirely. Generations of these people have lived here since the 1700s and earlier. They take heritage and bloodlines very seriously. Many are clannish, cliquish, slow to accept, and slow to forgive any indiscretion."

Raleigh chuckled, glad to be thinking about something besides Angelina. He was still smarting from her rejection, and he was doing his best to shut the memory of those blue-blue eyes from his mind.

"I can't believe it," he insisted, although he did remember some similar situations in his travels.

"Believe it, boy," Tod said, his eyes wide, his voice exaggerated in the southern manner. "Your problem is that you were California born and bred. This isn't California."

"Then why do you keep extolling the virtues of the place?" Raleigh asked seriously.

Tod grinned. "Ah, the *other* side of the story. We love it here, and we love the people generally. They'll stand by you through thick and thin once they accept you—*if* they accept you. I don't know what we would have done when we got flooded out two years ago if a lot of the townspeople hadn't pitched in and helped us clean up."

"You would have managed," Raleigh said. "If you'd told me, I would have sent money and hired help."

Carolyn patted his shoulder. "You do too much to help us as it is. We couldn't have bought the restaurant without your help."

"It was my pleasure," he said quietly.

Carolyn's eyes misted over. "You're a good brother, Raleigh." She looked embarrassed when he patted her cheek. "Well, I don't know about you two, but I'm beat. I'm going home to my bed. Between doing everything for this wedding, helping run this restaurant, and taking care of a ten-year-old, what I need is a month's vacation."

Raleigh grinned at her. "Poor Sis. Isn't the bride's family doing their share?"

She laughed. "The bride's family is in Italy. I'm"—
she looked at Tod—"*we're* doing the whole thing, including paying for it! Heaven forbid that we shouldn't
put on a show for this town, not to mention inviting as
many of them as we can! Thank God, the weather is
nice. We're going to set up tents in the park."

Raleigh laughed. "Will that get you in the clubs you
so covet, my dear?"

Carolyn pushed back her short blond hair. "Oh, you
two . . . stop teasing me! I'm making headway. Why,
just last week, Mrs. Teedell offered to sponsor me. Only
two more volunteer sponsors, and I'll be in."

They all laughed. Then Carolyn added seriously,
"Frankly, we've invited so many of the townspeople to
the wedding because they've been so supportive of the
restaurant. I don't need to remind you, Raleigh, that it
was touch and go when we moved here. We thought we
might lose the place before it gradually began to catch
on. As you know from your share of the profits, we're
doing nicely, very nicely indeed, and Tod and I want to
show our appreciation."

"What's the story on the bride's family?" Raleigh
asked. Carolyn hadn't mentioned them before.

She gave him her best martyred look. "Mimmi is one
of ten children. In fact, *she* sends money home to help
the family. She and Randolph are paying for the parents'
air fare so they can attend the wedding."

She shrugged. "What can I say? If we don't do the
wedding, there won't be anything but a simple civil ceremony. She's a sweetheart, a good worker for us, and
both she and Randolph deserve the best we can give
them."

"Spoken like a true mother," Raleigh teased. "And," he added, "not to be outdone, the uncle is going to do his part, too. What would you like me to do?"

"Nothing," Tod and Carolyn insisted in unison. "I told you that you do too much already," Carolyn added.

"Ah, but I've got to see that my big sis mixes with the cream of the southern crop," Raleigh insisted. "Now, how can I ensure that this is the wedding of the year—maybe the decade? Who's catering it? The restaurant?"

"Oh, good heavens, no!" Carolyn cried in mock alarm. "I've already said I have more to do than I can handle. Besides, catering our own wedding would be in decidedly poor taste. I'm having the best—the only possible—caterer in town, Valentine Smith, do it. I'm leaving it mostly in her hands."

Raleigh arched his brows. "Obviously she's capable, so what's your big problem?"

"The catering," Carolyn shot back at him, laughing at his naiveté. "Even with Valentine, I still have to consult with her on particulars, food and such, you know, how many people, that kind of thing."

"Why can't the bride do that?" Raleigh asked.

Carolyn rolled her eyes. "Good heavens, Raleigh, when you met the darling girl, didn't you notice that she speaks only twenty words of English?"

She laughed suddenly. "No, I don't suppose you did, since you spoke with her in Italian. Well, most of us are not blessed with being fluent in three languages. Anyway, the fact of the matter is that if we hadn't hired her to work in the kitchen and Randolph hadn't fallen in love with her, she'd have been sent back to Italy for sure by now."

"Oh, I see," Raleigh murmured.

"Then you also see what else that means, don't you? I have to help her select everything—the church, the flowers, her wedding gown, not to mention helping Randolph decide on his tux. I have to help with the bridesmaids' clothes—"

She put her hand on her head and moaned. "And they haven't found anywhere to live after they're married. Oh, thank God, I have only one other child left to marry off, and Tina's only ten."

Raleigh tugged on Carolyn's curls. "Let me make some of this easier for you like the good brother I am," he said, smiling at her.

"Like what?" she asked.

"I'll work with the caterer," he said.

"Are you crazy?" she asked. "What do you know about catering weddings?"

He leaned close and murmured, "My dear sister, I'll bet I've been to more weddings than you've ever even heard of. I've participated in weddings involving everything from beggars to kings. I do know something about them. And catering, too. Leave it to me. I promise you won't be disappointed. You've said yourself, you have enough to do."

"Weddings you may know about," she conceded, "but not southern weddings."

"I don't need to know about those. The caterer is the expert. In fact, I'll bet if you didn't try to stick your pert nose into every little detail, she'd do a much better job for you."

"Oh, I don't know about that, Raleigh," she said hesitantly.

"Not to worry at any rate," he insisted. "Give me the guest list and the other particulars relevant to the food, and I'll supervise."

"Are you sure?" she asked.

"I'm sure."

Carolyn couldn't hide her growing relief. She would be glad to be rid of any details; running back and forth to the bakery was one of her biggest headaches.

"Well, if you can help Carolyn out so easily, why couldn't you hire those belly dancers for me?" Tod teased.

"I really don't think the belly dancers would go over in mixed company," Carolyn interjected. "This place isn't ready for them."

"You didn't see these two," Tod insisted. "They were a comedy team and just about the funniest thing I've ever seen."

"They're not a comedy team anymore," Raleigh said tersely. "Straight belly dancing is all you would be able to get. Farrah—Tricia Haldran—said she would be happy to dance with her regular partner, Pat; however, Angelina was only a substitute," he said, hoping to dismiss the subject entirely.

"No fooling?" Tod said, his eyes twinkling. "Then Angelina really *was* that bad? She wasn't a comedy dancer after all?"

Raleigh shrugged. "I guess not, but as long as they entertained the guests, that's all I cared about."

Tod laughed. "Do you mean someone finally pulled

something over on you, Raleigh? You paid for what you didn't get?"

Again those blue eyes and wisps of blond hair flashed into Raleigh's mind. "Oh, I don't know," he mused. "I felt I got my money's worth. Didn't you?"

Tod slapped him on the back. "They were a riot, I agree. It's just a shame that they aren't really a comedy team. I had high hopes of having them dance at the restaurant."

"I still say it wouldn't work," Carolyn insisted. "I don't think this town is ready for belly dancers, period, except for small groups of women doing it in the dance studio for exercise. We just voted out the blue law, for heaven's sakes. Belly dancers for regular entertainment? No way!"

Raleigh smiled, glad for a chance to change the subject. "The blue law? You're not serious. What is it?"

"It means that only certain stores can open on Sundays," Carolyn explained with a smile. "That's how traditional the area is. There's strength and solidarity here—and resistance to change."

"No fooling?" Raleigh asked.

"No fooling," Carolyn repeated. "You just haven't learned much about this town yet."

"I've learned enough to know that we want to have a wedding that'll set the town on its ear," Raleigh teased, "so that my big sister can become part of the elite."

Both men laughed and Raleigh tousled her hair again until she blushed and protested, "Stop that, Raleigh, for heaven's sake."

"Tell me where the bakery is," he said, "and leave the rest to me."

"Right on Main Street," Tod told him. "You can't miss it, or the little lady who runs it. She bakes rolls for us. She's up at four in the morning, busy as a little beaver with that shop of hers."

Raleigh had a sudden memory of Angelina saying she got up early every morning; he dismissed it as abruptly as it had come. He'd seen few bakers who could resist their own products. He suspected the "little lady" was a lot larger than Angelina. But then it wouldn't take much to be larger than the dancer. She had been a slender little thing.

He shoved the thought from his mind. It would suit him just fine if he never encountered her again. He still felt rebuffed by her words. It had been years since a woman had dismissed him so curtly. He hoped it would be years before it happened again.

"Will you really take care of the catering?" Carolyn asked, afraid to believe her good fortune. "The wedding date is so close and there's so much to do. It would be such a relief."

Raleigh reached over and kissed his sister on the cheek. "For you, Sis, I'd do anything."

"Are you sure you know enough about it, Raleigh?" she pressed, doubt still on her face.

"Woman, I've dined with some of the *world's* elite!" he retorted, pretending to be insulted. "I surely know how to lay out a spread for a small southern town."

Carolyn laughed delightedly. "You're on, then, you're on. Let's see what you can do."

On Monday morning, bright and early, Raleigh set about making good his promise to his sister. He found the bakery easy enough, just as Tod had said he would.

When he entered, a stout, middle-aged woman behind the counter asked, "May I help you?"

Raleigh smiled. This was, no doubt, the "little lady" who ran the bakery.

"Yes," he said, extending his hand. "I'm Raleigh Coseegan, Carolyn Duncan's brother. I wanted to talk to you about catering the Domini-Duncan wedding."

The woman laughed cheerfully. "Oh, you'll be wanting Miss Valentine Smith. I'm Lucy Hassett, her helper. She's not in right now, but she should be back any minute."

Raleigh looked around the shop, seeing that the large room was cheerfully decorated in yellow-and-white polka dot wallpaper with a sunny linoleum floor. Half a dozen small round tables covered with yellow oilcloths sat along one wall. Their matching white wrought iron chairs had plump yellow cushions.

When he scanned the display counter, noting the assortment of sweets and breads, Lucy said, "Why don't you just sit down and have a cup of coffee and a sweet roll while you wait, Mr. Coseegan?"

He smiled. "Sounds like a good idea to me, Lucy. I think I'll have a jelly doughnut *and* a bear claw." He gestured toward a table in the corner. "May I sit there and eat them?"

"Yes, of course. That's why those tables are there." She wrapped the pastry in pieces of thin white paper and handed them to him. "How do you like your coffee?"

"Black."

"Fine. You go on and sit down and I'll bring the coffee to the table," she said with a motherly smile.

"Thank you," he replied, liking her already.

He settled comfortably into a chair, watching as Lucy fixed the coffee and brought it over. "How long have you worked here, Lucy?"

She laughed. "Good heavens! You don't want to know. If I tell that, I'll be telling my age. I've been here as long as I've held a job."

He grinned winningly at her. "You can't be more than forty. You must have been here twenty years."

"Pshaw! I'll never see fifty again. I've been here for thirty-five years, ever since old Mr. Rowland opened this bakery."

He laughed. "I can't believe it. Does Mr. Rowland still own it?"

She shook her head, then turned back to the counter as some customers came into the room, causing the bell over the door to jingle. "Excuse me," she murmured politely.

When she had waited on the customers and they had gone, she came back to stand by Raleigh's table. "Miss Smith's the owner." Lucy smiled. "As sweet a girl as you'd ever want to meet. New to town, and bless her little heart, all alone."

Before Raleigh could comment, Lucy spoke again. "But then, you are too, aren't you?"

Taken aback by her direct question, he nodded. Was his loneliness evident these days? "I've never married."

Lucy laughed. "My goodness, I wasn't asking that. I meant that you're new to town."

Raleigh laughed deeply. "Forgive me. Being a bachelor, I'm used to people trying to find me a wife. I just naturally thought you were asking my marital status."

Lucy chuckled good-naturedly. "I take it you don't want a wife."

He was pensive for a moment. It was a question he'd given a lot of thought to recently. He didn't think he wanted a wife, yet when a man began to wonder, who could say?

"Not at the moment," he finally replied, "and yes, I am new in town. I'm here for my nephew Randolph Duncan's wedding."

"Why, yes, I know. You're the writer brother."

Raleigh smiled. "I guess that's me."

"We're so excited about doing that wedding," Lucy said enthusiastically. "The cake is going to be wonderful. Miss Smith's doing the decorating of it herself, and is she talented! She went to some fancy cooking school in Washington, D.C., and you should see some of the things she does."

"Oh?" he murmured.

"Yes, indeed. We've got all kinds of ideas for the little cakes Mrs. Duncan wants, and we're going to make some kind of noodle pudding with a foreign name as a special treat for the bride and the relatives who're coming from overseas."

"What's the name of it?" he asked, interested.

Lucy's laughter held a hint of embarrassment. "I can't pronounce it very well, but Miss Smith knows how to make it—looken krodel, or something like that."

"Ah," he said.

Lucy nodded. "And of course, we're making the bread fresh, too. Rolls for small sandwiches—sort of like the ones we do for the breakfast crowd at the restaurant."

Raleigh's brows arched ever so slightly. Tod had said Valentine did business with the restaurant, too. She sounded like a hard worker.

"Course those were made by her, too."

"I beg your pardon," he said, losing the train of conversation.

"Those doughnuts you're eating. They were baked by Miss Smith."

"Oh?" he murmured. "They're delicious. Does she do all the cooking?"

"More than the poor little thing should," Lucy said with a sympathetic sigh. "She comes in here at four every morning to get her work done. Although Junior Hampton helps her, he goes home at noon. Bless her heart, the dear is here until we close every evening."

Raleigh nodded sympathetically. "She does sound like she puts in some long hours."

"She does indeed. I told her, 'Honey, you're only twenty-five years old. You go out and have yourself some fun.' But what can she do? Mr. Carruthers raised the rent last month, and by fifty dollars, too." She shook her head and put her hands on her hips. "And there was no cause, I can tell you."

Raleigh frowned. "Don't they get along?"

"Humph! Get along?"

The bell tingled again and a young woman rushed into the room like a whirlwind. Raleigh set down his coffee cup and stared at her as his mind spun dizzily.

The woman was blond, slender, shapely, and she had

the bluest eyes he'd ever seen—except on the dancer
Angelina.

"How's business, Lucy?" Valentine called out, as she
put a small box on the nearest table.

"Fine," Lucy said cheerfully.

Valentine's voice was animated, her eyes all aglow.
"Just wait until you see the new recipes I found!" she
exclaimed excitedly.

When she turned to look at Lucy, she saw the man at
the last table and sucked in her breath sharply. Raleigh
Coseegan himself! She didn't believe it! And in her
shop. She felt her face flame as she met his bold, pene-
trating gaze.

"Good morning," she said crisply, all the cheerful-
ness evaporating from her voice.

Raleigh grinned. He would recognize that tart voice
anywhere. This was the elusive Angelina, as sure as he
was Raleigh Coseegan. Suddenly it all fell into place so
nicely: the disguise; the reason she didn't want anyone
to know who she was; her apparent need for money,
about which Lucy had informed him.

But he wasn't about to tip his hat. There was plenty
of time for that later. He had better sense than to put her
on the defensive. He *still* wanted to know her.

"Good morning. You must be Valentine Smith."

Valentine tried to still the hammering of her heart.
How did he know? Surely he hadn't found out that she
was Angelina. Tricia had promised!

She swallowed with difficulty. "Yes, I'm Valentine
Smith. Who are you?" She wasn't foolish enough to let
on that she knew who he was.

Standing up, Raleigh held out his hand. "I'm Raleigh

Coseegan. I understand you're catering the Domini-Duncan wedding. Carolyn's my sister. She sent me over to get to know you since I'll be helping with the wedding arrangements."

"Excuse me," Lucy said, "I've got to see to something in the oven."

Neither Raleigh nor Valentine seemed to notice the woman as she walked away. Valentine wasn't about to let Raleigh clasp her fingers in his. She recalled all too well the sensations he created inside her with only his nearness.

Ignoring his outstretched hand, she tried to decide what to do. She couldn't believe her horrid luck. The bride's family usually handled the wedding, but the bride in this case was from Italy and now living here alone. She was happily letting Mrs. Duncan handle most of the details. Wouldn't that be the way of it with this wedding, of all weddings!

"I trust there's nothing wrong with Mrs. Duncan," Valentine said with a frown. "She's been working with me herself."

"Not a thing wrong with my sister," Raleigh replied, smiling broadly. He intended to erase Valentine's frown completely. "She's just so busy with the restaurant, and she thought I might prove beneficial."

"I see," she murmured. What else could she say? She literally couldn't afford to offend the Duncans.

Raleigh's appreciative gaze raced over Valentine. Nice, very nice. She was even more refreshing than he had anticipated. Wholesome, young, and pretty.

"And what specifically can I help you with now?" Valentine asked, forcing the words from her mouth. She wouldn't let herself remember that this man had laughed at her, any more than she'd let herself remember that she was silly enough to find him attractive. "We won't be doing the baking until the week of the wedding, of course."

"You can have dinner with me tomorrow night."

She widened her eyes. "Really, I don't think that's necessary." She had enough sense to have as little to do with him as possible.

He smiled. "We have catering business to discuss. Why not discuss it over a pleasant meal? I understand you have some clever ideas for the food my sister has ordered."

Valentine pulled out the other chair and sat down. Making herself smile brightly, she said, "I have time right now to discuss that with you, Mr. Coseegan."

"Please, make that Raleigh," he urged, smiling winningly.

He took another sip of his coffee, then set the cup down. "You aren't one of those women who turns down every dinner invitation, are you, Valentine?" he asked, causing her heartbeats to increase. Did he know she was Angelina? If not, she certainly didn't want him drawing any parallels.

"Even though it is business?" he continued.

She shook her head hurriedly. "No, of course not."

"Good," he said, "because unfortunately I can't stay right now. Seven o'clock tomorrow night for dinner? Where do you live?"

Pressing her lips into a thin line, Valentine considered her options. Apparently Mrs. Duncan *had* sent him. And he was as persistent as ever. She might as well have dinner with him and get it over with.

"Why don't I meet you at the restaurant?" she asked, making herself smile again.

"At the family's restaurant?"

She nodded.

"I don't think so. I eat there so often. I'm sure you understand. I'll pick you up and we can decide then."

"Fine!" she said more sharply than she had intended. First Mr. Carruthers. Now Raleigh Coseegan. He wasn't giving her any chance to keep her distance from him. She was beginning to think she liked him better when he was laughing at her. At least she didn't have to deal with him personally.

When she had marched over to the cash register, she grabbed up a piece of paper and dashed off her address. "I'm sure you can find it," she said curtly.

He winked. "I'm sure I can. I've managed to find my way all over the world."

She nodded, folding her arms and watching as he flashed her another smile and walked out.

" 'I've managed to find my way all over the world,' " she mimicked. "Whoopee for you, Mr. Big Shot."

"Handsome, isn't he?" Lucy asked, coming out of the kitchen to watch Raleigh walk down the street.

"Handsome?" Valentine repeated, looking over her shoulder at Lucy. She glanced back out the window at Raleigh. "Oh, I suppose so," she grudgingly agreed.

"I liked him," Lucy said. "He's real nice to be such an important person."

"Huh! Important person," Valentine muttered.

"He is," Lucy insisted. "He goes all over the world writing about the foreign wars and such. His stories are in a lot of the magazines my husband Arnie reads."

"I don't think he's such a big deal," Valentine insisted, turning away from the window. She glanced back one more time.

He really was handsome—one of the most attractive men she had ever seen. And she was afraid she did think he was a big deal, a very big deal.

Oh, Lord, what was she going to do? How could she work with him and still keep out of harm's way during the time Raleigh would be here?

CHAPTER FOUR

VALENTINE COULDN'T BELIEVE how rapidly the next day passed. Of course, she was always so busy that time flew, but this day seemed to go by faster than the others. She tried to keep her mind off Raleigh Coseegan, which proved impossible, no matter how hard she worked. The same thing had happened when she tried to get to sleep last night.

Cross, tired, and irritable because she had stewed about him half the night, she found herself even more resentful of the position she was in as her workday ended. She didn't want to subject herself to Raleigh Coseegan. She doubted very seriously that he was used to helping out with weddings, no matter how stressed and busy his sister was.

She was sure his basic reason for insisting upon working with her on the catering was because he wasn't

used to women saying no to him. When she'd said it, he
had seemed genuinely surprised. Well, she wished she'd
been in the position of giving him even more of a surprise: she wished she had been able to tell him she
would not go to dinner with him—*period*!

Unfortunately, all too soon, it was time to go home
and get dressed for her dinner date with him. *Appointment!* she quickly amended. She wasn't going on a *date*
with Raleigh. This was strictly business. What on earth
was she thinking?

To her utter chagrin and dismay, she realized in one
swift moment what it was: even though she felt as if she
had been coerced into this evening, she was unable to
suppress a small flare of excitement at the thought of
seeing Raleigh again. It had been so long since she'd
gotten the slightest bit interested in any man.

Brady had burned her so badly with his shocking be-
trayal and lies that she didn't know if she could ever
trust another man. And to begin with Raleigh Coseegan!
It was absurd! If ever a man had "Warning: danger
ahead" written all over him, this one did.

At her small cottage, she fussed and fumed about
what to wear. She kept telling herself that it didn't really
matter, that she should just throw on whatever; yet each
time she pulled one of her dresses from a hanger, she
quickly hung it back up again.

"Darn!" she muttered aloud.

This was ridiculous. Really, anything would be fine.
She still had all the dresses she had purchased when she
worked at the bank, and they were basically nice, neat
business dresses. That was just it, she told herself, she
wanted something special.

The idea startled her. She *didn't* want something special, she reminded herself sharply. Never mind that Raleigh Coseegan was attractive and worldly. A business dress was precisely what was required for dinner this evening to discuss the Domini-Duncan wedding. She was too smart to be carrying on like this over a man who could be nothing but trouble.

She grabbed up the next dress in the line and laid it out on her bed. When she had found matching heels, she went to the bathroom and took a leisurely shower.

She was used to wearing her long blond hair pinned up for work at the bakery, but tonight she toyed with wearing it down. At last she hastily put it in a chignon at the back of her neck and completed the finishing touches of her makeup.

She really didn't even like Raleigh Coseegan, she thought, remembering what he'd said about taking his laughs where he found them. And, she reminded herself firmly, she and her belly dance had been one of his laughs, whether he realized it or not. With a sudden pang of alarm, she wondered if he had discovered that she was the belly dancer.

She sighed. Ever since Brady, she'd been overly suspicious of all men. And with reason! Excitement and resentment mingled with her fear that Raleigh really did know who she was. Yet how would he? Still, she simply couldn't bear it if he did. She wanted to forget that dance ever existed.

She was all in a dither over the entire matter when her doorbell rang. It gave her the incentive she needed to put on a cool, businesslike façade.

That façade almost failed her when she opened the

door to find Raleigh in a sexy white summer suit with a two-tone brown shirt that set off his dancing dark eyes.

"Well, good evening," he murmured in a deep cultured voice that immediately made Val's nerve endings tingle. Oh, Lord, she told herself, why couldn't he look like a toad and sound like one too?

"Hello," she said, a trifle more coolly than she had intended. She was throwing up armor in all directions, trying valiantly to protect herself from this man, no matter what his real reasons for being here tonight. She realized she was more afraid of herself than of him.

Raleigh didn't miss any of her signals. She meant to keep her distance from him; he meant to see that didn't happen.

Something about this pretty blonde made him want to take her in his arms and tell her that he could, and would make her happy. She had barely hidden vulnerability in her sky blue eyes and pretty, guarded features.

But it was way too soon for the kind of thinking he was doing, for her *and* for him. Still, he liked what he saw. She had a freshness that he hadn't encountered in a long, long time. The women he usually spent time with —and there had been many, maybe too many—were sophisticated, generally wealthy, with a ready wit and experience and background that often matched his own.

This woman appeared to be sheltered and untouched by the hard, cruel world that existed beyond this small town. He was willing to bet that the worst thing that had happened to her was a broken heart. She was wary of him. Of that he had no doubt.

Of course he didn't know her. In his business, however, he had learned to read people well, and he believed his assessment of her was accurate. His ability to judge character had often meant the difference between life and death in a country at war, where one man willingly betrayed another for only a token fee.

Still, this wasn't war. In fact, it was the furthest thing from war that Raleigh could think of. Despite the simple blue dress and matching heels Valentine wore, and the severe hairstyle, he found her sexy and enchanting in an innocent way that seemed totally at odds with the term *sexy*.

She was so pretty and doll-like that the outfit itself just called attention to her charms. She could no more play the part of the severe spinster than she could belly dance. The idea amused him as a vision of her in that oversized costume flashed into his mind. Immediately, he felt himself responding to that picture of her.

"What's so funny, Mr. Coseegan?" Valentine asked tautly, extremely sensitive to any hint of being laughed at by this man.

Raleigh shook his head. "I'm just so delighted to see you," he improvised. "I was afraid you wouldn't be home. You were less than enthusiastic about dinner, yet here you are, looking absolutely delightful."

Automatically, Val looked down at her plain dress and wished she'd found something else. She could just imagine the women he usually went to dinner with: cosmopolitan, beautiful, exquisitely dressed and made-up.

When she glanced back up at Raleigh, she was embarrassed because she was sure he could tell what she was thinking.

"It's a very basic dress, a business dress," she said

defensively. "I worked in a bank before I opened the bakery."

She could feel the color rush to her cheeks. She wished to heaven she hadn't said *that*. Why mention that awful bank at all? What on earth was the matter with her? This man was going to be her undoing, she could sense it. But she didn't know what to do about it.

"I'm sure you brightened many a customer's day," Raleigh said flatteringly.

Valentine blushed again. This wasn't going to work at all. She felt like such a country bumpkin with this man, although she hadn't really considered herself one before. Sure, she was obviously gullible and naive for Brady to have been able to pull such a stunt over on her but hadn't she learned from that?

Just what *was* it she had learned? It had only taken her two years in a bank in Boston to learn enough to go running back to a small town to hide. She had returned to the kind of area she felt most comfortable in.

Having been raised by her grandfather in an isolated little North Carolina town, she couldn't wait to get to the big time after Grandpa died. But she had been burned, hurt, shamed, and very nearly shattered. So what were her lessons? Mistrust? Fear?

Standing here with Raleigh, she didn't feel she'd learned anything at all in her entire life. She was sure he was way out of her league. The best thing to do was get this darned catering business over with as quickly as possible and hope to heaven that he left town the minute the wedding was over!

"I think we should go," she announced abruptly. "As I've explained, I have to get up very early in the morn-

ing, and really, Mr. Coseegan, I don't see the need for
this dinner tonight. People usually discuss business with
me in the shop."

"Oh?" he murmured, his dark blond brows raised.
"Am I breaching small-town etiquette? If so, please forgive me. I'm a long way from home, and not used to
conducting business anywhere but over dinner."

Valentine didn't know if he was teasing her or not;
she was feeling more and more like a backwoods rube,
despite the time she'd lived in Boston.

"That's all right," she said crisply. "Everybody does
things differently everywhere, I'm sure. When I was in
Boston . . ."

She let the words trail off. What was her obsession
with bringing up hints of that awful time around this
man? Was it because she had been so humiliated on
stage, belly dancing, that the shame of the bank embez-
zlement flooded her mind and wouldn't leave?

He gave her a heartstopping smile. "Thank you for
understanding."

Her hand on the knob, ready to close the door, Val
pushed past him. "Shall we go?"

Looking a little amused, Raleigh wrapped his fingers
around hers and pulled the door closed. Valentine spun
around to look at him.

"Two things," he said softly. "Part of the charm of a
small southern town is supposed to be the slow pace.
Could we slow things down just a bit? And could you
please stop calling me Mr. Coseegan?" He grinned at
her. "It makes me feel so old, and even though I am
feeling my age, I don't like to be reminded of it."

Valentine stared at the dashing man before her. Ra-

leigh Coseegan old? The idea was preposterous. He was
the best-looking man she'd seen in she couldn't remember when. Maybe all of her life. In spite of his
worldly demeanor and the wisdom in his eyes, she'd be
surprised if he was a day over thirty.

"I'm sure you haven't seen thirty-two yet," she said
dryly. "You're hardly old."

"I'll bet you a birthday cake, which you have to
bake, that I'm older than you think," he said impulsively. It would be one more way to get to see her,
regardless of whether she guessed accurately or not. Although he couldn't help recalling how old he'd felt at
Randolph's bachelor party, he was well aware that he
looked much younger than he was.

Valentine didn't want any more to do with Raleigh
than she could avoid. Why on earth would she be foolish enough to wager with him?

She shook her head. "I don't bet."

"Come on," he teased, charm oozing from every
pore. "Just one cake. I can't recall the last time someone made a birthday cake for me. If you guess wrong, I
get the cake free. If I lose, I want the biggest birthday
cake you bake, and I'll buy it. My birthday's coming up
in two weeks—the day Randolph's getting married.
You can't lose either way."

Valentine looked at him again. Why did he want her
to bet with him? Was he older than he looked? Was he
searching for a compliment because he looked so good
for his age?

Sighing in resignation, she decided she might as well
get this over with, too. She was sure she was right anyway. He was tanned and sun-lined, but surely this man

couldn't be over thirty-five. She was perfectly safe in making the bet with him. Anyway, she knew that he was younger than Carolyn Duncan, who Trish had told her was thirty-nine.

"To be honest," she felt obliged to say, "I know that you're Mrs. Duncan's younger brother. I also know she's thirty-nine. You're no more than thirty-five."

"You will bake the cake yourself if you lose, won't you?" Raleigh asked.

Valentine nodded. "Who else? I'm the baker, along with one primary helper. I sure wouldn't give the business to my competition. But, I warn you, my cakes are some of the most expensive in town."

Raleigh smiled confidently. "We'll settle this bet while we eat our dinner, lady."

"All right." Valentine felt certain she wouldn't lose. The man looked too good to be any older than thirty. In fact, he was probably about twenty-eight or twenty-nine. He really was handsome. She wished she wouldn't keep thinking that.

To her surprise, he drove to a town twenty-five miles away. Valentine had never been there. Raleigh obviously had found his way around in the short time he'd been in Virginia, for he drove unerringly to the restaurant.

"Do you visit with your sister often?" she asked, curiosity getting the better of her.

He shook his head. "Only three times in the seven years they've been in the South."

"Oh."

"So how did I know about this restaurant?" he said, asking the question she wanted to ask. "I'm the restless kind, and when I come to town, I travel to the surrounding areas, investigating, checking places out. After all, that's how I make my living," he said with a grin. "I'm nosy. And," he added with a chuckle, "I love to try out new restaurants. Have you been here before?"

Valentine shook her head. "I'm afraid I don't get around much myself. My hours, you know," she added.

Of course that wasn't exactly all the truth. She was still keeping a low profile, hoping her past didn't follow her. The fewer contacts she made outside town, the safer she felt.

"I think you'll like this," Raleigh said. "If you like Italian food. It's quite authentic."

"I love Italian," she admitted, smiling a little for the first time. She hadn't had any good pasta since she left Boston. She and Brady had often lunched at a favorite Italian place.

Brady again, she thought, the memory causing her stomach to churn uncomfortably. Suddenly she didn't even think she could eat Italian food, much less enjoy it.

"The fettuccine here is delicious," Raleigh said, climbing out of the car.

Fettuccine, Valentine thought: her very favorite. Or at least it had been. She and Brady had usually shared a big plate and antipasto. She looked up sharply when Raleigh opened the door for her and held out his hand.

Oh, but he was smooth, she told herself. When he clasped her fingers warmly, she felt the heat all the way to the core of her being. No man had touched her intimately in months. And this man of all men had to be the first!

To her dismay, he tucked her arm beneath his after he had helped her from the car. Valentine fought the urge to draw away.

His nearness stirred her senses wildly. She couldn't keep from feeling a little bit proud walking beside Raleigh Coseegan when they entered the restaurant. He was the kind of man who commanded attention; she didn't miss the way people were staring at him. It was more than just local curiosity about a stranger, and Raleigh seemed quite comfortable with it.

But then why shouldn't he be? Valentine asked herself, suddenly coming back to reality. He was world famous. He was used to attention.

"Good evening," he said warmly to the hostess who came to seat them.

The tall, dark brunette flirted with him unabashedly, totally ignoring Valentine.

"Good evening, Mr. Coseegan. How good to see you again so soon! Mama's cooking must agree with you."

Raleigh easily and casually returned her warmth. "Indeed it does. Your place is the best Italian restaurant I've found in the South. Please be sure to tell your mother so."

He gently ushered Valentine forward with his hand at the back of her waist. "Everything is so delicious that I wanted my lady to try it," he said. "She owns a bakery, so she's a woman who appreciates good food and the work involved."

Valentine felt a shiver up and down her spine, not only from Raleigh's warm touch, but from his compliment and his calling her his lady. She was so distracted that she didn't even notice the sulky pout the other woman gave him.

"Mama will be real pleased when I tell her you're here. Will you stay and talk with us tonight when she gets a break?"

Raleigh winked at Valentine, causing her heartbeat to accelerate. "Not tonight. I'm taking my lady for a country drive."

Looking decidedly disappointed, the hostess said, "Oh," and led them to a table beside a tall window overlooking a beautiful rose garden.

"Thank you, Genna. This is marvelous," Raleigh said.

Genna managed a strained smile before placing two menus on the table.

"Would you like to start with wine?" Raleigh asked, pulling Valentine's chair out for her. He was so close that she could feel his breath on her cheek as he helped seat her.

Oh, dear! she thought. Wine loosened her tongue terribly, and she needed all her wits about her to get through this meal with this fascinating man. Yes, she repeated to herself, Raleigh Coseegan was fascinating indeed, and she had only been with him half an hour.

"Yes, please," she heard herself say, as though her brain hadn't just issued a fervent warning.

She listened while Raleigh ordered a special vintage. She really didn't know anything about wines. She and Brady had gotten the house wine every time. Brady again! she thought irritably. Why did he keep intruding on her thoughts?

When Genna had gone, Raleigh lightly touched Valentine's hand to get her attention. She looked at him, startled. She hadn't realized that she was gazing distractedly around the room.

"I hope the restaurant is all right," he murmured, his warm fingers teasingly tracing hers.

"It's fine," she all but stammered. Lord, this man was a charmer! She felt another shiver race over her.

"You have such lovely skin," he whispered, "so soft and fair."

It was all Valentine could do not to snatch her hand back. "Thank you," she replied, the crispness returning to her voice as she slowly slid her fingers from his and picked up the menu with both hands.

Raleigh studied her for a moment as she pretended total concentration in the selection. Long lashes shielded her blue eyes; she had the most charming blush on her pale cheeks. She was going to take a lot of work to win over, but he suspected she would be worth it.

"Will you share the antipasto with me?" he asked after a minute.

Valentine's blue gaze darted up to meet his dark one. "Yes, that will be fine."

"I'm having the fettuccine," he added. "Have you decided?"

Valentine put her menu down; she had known all along that she would have fettuccine, too.

"I'll have the same," she said.

Genna returned to the table with a bottle of wine. Valentine watched, intrigued, as Raleigh sampled a little and approved it. Val was surprised to find a restaurant in this small town that stood on ceremony. Even at the restaurant where she ate in Boston, the wine had simply been delivered and perfunctorily served. Glancing at Raleigh, she found herself wondering if this was standard treatment, or if it was special for him.

"Excellent!" he announced. "Absolutely excellent."

Genna grinned. "Mama said you would like it." She set the bottle down in the stand and touched Raleigh's shoulder with a long-nailed hand. "Mama also said you must at least come back to the kitchen and speak to her."

Smiling, Raleigh agreed. Then he placed their order. When Genna had written it down, she waited for him to follow her. Impatience flashed across her face when he leaned over Valentine to slide back her chair. Val was almost tempted to refuse, but clearly Raleigh intended that she go.

In the kitchen, she met a round, friendly Italian woman named Maria who spoke limited English. She and Raleigh spoke briefly in Italian, then he introduced Valentine, again noting that she ran a bakery.

"She's catering my nephew's wedding," he added. "She's going to serve all sorts of dishes. The bride and her family are from Italy."

"No!" Maria exclaimed. "They are who? Maybe I know these people."

When Raleigh told her, Maria asked where they lived and an animated conversation ensued, with the two of them reverting to Italian. Ultimately Maria decided she didn't know the other Italians. She, however, was delighted to be issued a wedding invitation all the same. She turned to Valentine.

"We must talk about the recipes!" she said excitedly.

"Mine is—" At a loss for words, she kissed her finger-tips.

Valentine laughed. "I'd love to know how you make it."

"Tonight you will try it. Yes, I insist," Maria said. "For the wedding, I insist. And so I will help you to make it." She looked embarrassed. "If it's okay, I insist."

Valentine laughed again. "I'd be honored, I assure you. Thank you."

"Okay, then we settle it. Go. I will fix your food. Then we talk."

Raleigh reached out and playfully patted Maria's cheek. "But only for a while. I'm taking my lady for a moonlight ride after dinner."

Maria's dark eyes twinkled. "Ah. The moonlight ride. Is love, no?"

When Valentine looked embarrassed and tried valiantly to think of what to say, Raleigh took her arm and escorted her from the kitchen without explaining that they were really here on business. In fact, she realized, she'd almost forgotten it herself! Raleigh and his moonlight ride indeed!

After he had once again seated her, she placed both hands on the table and locked her fingers together so there would be no chance of his stroking them again.

"Now, Raleigh, about the catering—"

His dark eyes met hers. "Yes?" he asked calmly. Then he proceeded to pour her a glass of wine.

"Exactly what is it you want to discuss?" she murmured, words suddenly failing her as he handed her the goblet.

"Well," he said, pausing to sip his wine, "cost isn't the issue here. We want something memorable, something special. After all, a wedding should be as romantic as possible, don't you think? Love is so rare. So magical. I can look at Randolph and Mimmi and see the joy they find in each other."

"Why, yes," she murmured, surprised that this bold, worldly man would speak of romance so poetically.

"Have you met the bride?" he asked.

"Only briefly," Valentine said. "Mrs. Duncan brought her into the shop. She seemed very shy and she spoke so little English that it was difficult to communicate with her."

"Yes," Raleigh said, smiling. "But isn't she delightful?"

Valentine nodded. "She is." Her eyes met his. "Have you ever been married, Raleigh?"

He laughed openly and Valentine was once more embarrassed. She had spoken before she'd thought. Although she had been dying to know, she wouldn't have asked for all the world.

He shook his head. "I'm afraid I'm a bit cynical about marriage," he admitted. "However, I do greatly admire the beauty of the union and the hope behind the idea. When I attend the joining of a man and a woman in holy matrimony, it's always my fervent wish that the marriage will live to fulfill the promise of the vows. I certainly hope so for Randolph and Mimmi. All too often, marriage is a surprise and a disappointment to both parties."

Well, so much for thinking of him as romantic, Valentine told herself, sobering suddenly.

"Have you been married?" he asked, startling her. Even though she'd asked him, she hadn't expected the question.

She shook her head, thinking once more of Brady. They'd been engaged for over a year. *Engaged!* And he'd still deceived her in the worst possible way.

"Ah, but I'll bet you've come close—a pretty little southern belle like you," he murmured.

Valentine laughed. "I suppose I am a southern belle since I was raised in North Carolina, but I did spend some time in Boston. I've only been in town six months myself."

There she went again, she told herself, bringing up Boston. But Raleigh didn't seem to pay any attention. Delighted to hear her bright laughter, he smiled warmly.

"You have all the old traditional traits one expects in a southern belle. Ladylike, Quiet. Reserved. Concerned with appearances. And very, very sweet when you're not using that tart tongue on me. Those things must be bred through the generations in some southern females."

Being a southern belle actually sounded boring, Valentine thought, but it sure beat being thought of as a criminal. Or a belly dancer! She looked down at her wineglass, then took another sip despite herself. It was beginning to relax her, and she was anxious to keep her thoughts in order.

"I have to be concerned with appearances," she said softly. "My business is the most important thing in my life, and I'm still trying to make inroads into established bakeries that have been in town for generations."

Raleigh waited until she set her glass down, then reached across and cupped her chin, making her look at him. "Valentine Smith, you don't have a worry in this world. The town, especially the people who frequent Tod and Carolyn's restaurant, think your bakery goods are something exceptional."

"Thank you." She reached up to remove his hand, and he caught her fingers in his.

"I think you're something exceptional, too," he murmured.

Valentine was doing everything she could not to succumb to this man's relentless flattery, yet she couldn't help taking pleasure in it. She didn't want to be a fool —heaven knows she didn't—but she'd needed a man's attention for a long while.

Right in the nick of time, Genna appeared with the antipasto, loudly setting the platter down, jarring Valentine back to reality. What on earth was she doing daydreaming about this roving Romeo? He was only in town for a short time.

If she weren't very, very careful, he could do as much damage to her as Brady had done. Already he was starting little flames inside her, the likes of which Brady hadn't kindled in the entire two years she'd known him.

"Your dinner will be here in a few minutes," Genna said, smiling once again at Raleigh, her pique seemingly evaporated, no doubt by order of Mama's tongue.

"About the catering for the wedding," Valentine began again. "Just what did you have in mind?"

Damn, Raleigh thought to himself, he'd lost her again. He was beginning to hate the crisp sound that slipped into her voice so easily.

He smiled. "What Carolyn really wants is to set the town on its ear," he said, winking conspiratorially. "Of course, as I said, of primary importance is that this wedding be romantic, a rich theme of love that crosses cultural and geographical boundaries; we all think a mix of Italian and southern food would be nice. And some custom mingling wouldn't hurt."

He leaned forward. "Of course, the custom part won't be your job, although I think it would be beneficial if we all worked closely together—florist, caterer, the bride and groom, the family, and you and I."

Valentine sighed. The wedding really was beginning to take on a new flavor. She had known it was going to be a big undertaking, an important job for her; but until Raleigh stated it so clearly—and eloquently—she hadn't seen just what a wonderful opportunity this was. Even though Carolyn had rushed by the shop several times, they hadn't gotten down to basics as Raleigh had.

Valentine met his dark eyes. She was really looking forward to this job. She felt confident she could handle it, and she would have fun working with the florist, matching colors and themes. She liked the Duncan family, and she had found Mimmi sweet.

The only problem she was having was the idea of working closely with Raleigh. Oh, Lord, was she having a problem with that!

CHAPTER FIVE

"WHAT DO YOU think?" Raleigh asked, drawing Valentine back to the topic at hand.

"I think it's grand," she answered honestly, her mind already beginning to teem with ideas for mixing traditional southern foods with Italian. On confident ground, suddenly very exuberant about the prospects, she began to outline combinations that she thought would be tasty, innovative, decorative, and memorable.

Raleigh smiled. She was in her glory talking about cooking, her blue eyes bright and her pretty features animated. She gestured extravagantly with her small, delicate hands.

His gaze strayed down the plain dress and he remembered how slender and cute she'd been in that belly-dance costume. And sexy. He wished he could forget that, but, sitting across from her now, it simply wasn't possible. He wondered how it would be to take her in his arms. He could almost taste her kisses. He could already imagine what it would be like to hold her body against his.

"Raleigh, what do you think? Does it sound good to you?"

He almost groaned. Wouldn't she be surprised to know what was on his mind? What he really thought? To know how good it did sound to him . . .

"Wonderful," he said, putting a big smile on his face and hoping he was saying the correct thing.

"I have a special old southern bread pudding in mind," she continued, almost breathlessly, caught up in the creations in her mind. "For color, I think traditional cherry cobbler is called for. I hope cherry blossoms are going to be part of the flower arrangements. They're so delicate and romantic."

Raleigh, too, was caught up in the creations of his mind. He wanted to make love to this woman. He wanted to feel her heat and her enthusiasm when he caressed her body. He wanted her to exclaim over him as she was doing over the desserts she was planning for the wedding.

When he noticed that she was idly nibbling on odds and ends from the antipasto tray while she talked, he followed suit, although he really wasn't very hungry. He was finding Valentine more and more enchanting. He loved her passionate involvement in her work. He suspected she was equally passionate in everything—with the right partner. He wanted to be that partner.

It was true that he was much too cynical to believe in love at first sight, he told himself, but he did believe there was a time and a place for everything—a season, as it were. He abruptly thought his time and place, his season, were now, here, with Valentine Smith. He was a little taken aback by the suddenness, and he wanted to know more about her. Much more. He was a reckless man, it was true, but not when it came to his heart.

"Tell me how you came to Virginia and why you bought the bakery after having worked in a bank," he said.

Valentine had a sudden compulsion to be honest with him, yet she didn't dare. She didn't know him well enough. Anyway, there was no point in exposing her ugly past. He would be gone all too soon and she didn't want him left with doubts about her integrity.

"My grandfather owned a bakery when I was a child," she reminisced, a dreamy look entering her blue eyes. "It was literally his reason for living—the bakery and me," she added a little shyly.

Raleigh told himself that she would be a good reason for living. He could imagine that she had been a charming child.

"He spoiled me rotten, I'm afraid," Valentine continued. "My parents were very young, not married, and neither of them wanted me, but I didn't know it at the time. All I knew was that my grandfather loved me and cared for me. I didn't miss having a conventional home. We lived over the bakery. My childhood was full of the sights and sounds and smells of baked goods. Everyone loved Grandpa," she added, "not just me. He had a way with people."

"It sounds like a wonderful childhood," Raleigh said.

"It was," Valentine agreed. "Until Grandpa lost the

bakery. Even then I didn't know how devastating it was to him. We lived on his Social Security checks after that, and I didn't lack for anything. I was too young to know that his dream died with the bakery. He gave all of his time and attention to me then."

She glanced away. "I'm afraid he sheltered me too much. I didn't have a realistic concept of the world. Later I took care of Grandpa for several years, while working part time in a bank. When he died, I set out for the big city of Boston." She laughed a little bitterly. "It was fine for a while."

"Why only for a while?" Raleigh asked.

She shrugged again. "Things didn't go as I planned."

"Was there a man involved?" he asked gently.

Valentine couldn't know that her blue eyes were like an open book. She was surprised that Raleigh was so perceptive. How could he know? Had someone told him? Or was he just that clever?

"Oh, there were a few along the way," she said with pretended nonchalance. "Nothing really serious when I was younger." She smiled. "I was a late bloomer. Maybe Grandpa was afraid I'd make the same mistake Mama made. He was always cautioning me not to hurry love."

"I'm sure it was sound advice," Raleigh said with a smile. "You're very pretty. There must have been many men who wanted to hurry love with you." He knew he sure as hell did!

Valentine glanced away again. She'd never considered herself a great beauty by any stretch of the imagination. She'd always wished she was tall, like her mother. But once again, she was terribly flattered by Raleigh's words, foolishly flattered.

"What about your childhood?" she asked, wanting to get away from her own past.

He chuckled. "Nothing so nostalgic as yours," he answered. "Carolyn and I were rather spoiled, too, I'm afraid. My parents weren't wealthy, but they both worked and earned good incomes. We had everything we wanted. We were encouraged to live our lives. It was the California way," he added.

"Well, it seems you've certainly lived yours," Valentine couldn't resist saying. "You've done so much, traveled everywhere, written about everything. It sounds very fulfilling and exciting."

"It's had its moments," he said with a casual shrug. He had thought it was an incredible way of life at one time; he knew that he was very lucky to have been able to do what he wanted with his career. But that season seemed to be over, too.

Hell, he thought to himself, maybe he was just getting old. That reminded him of the bet he'd made with Valentine.

"About my birthday cake," he said, a wicked gleam suddenly brightening his dark eyes. "When are you going to bake it? Now it seems to me that we should celebrate the week before the wedding. I don't want to intrude on Randolph's big day, even though he did pick it because it's my birthday." He smiled. "To tell you the honest truth, I'm as flattered as I can be, too."

Valentine smiled. "Of course you are. It's an honor to you for him to want to be married on your birthday. But about that cake—I haven't lost the bet. You haven't shown me anything to indicate your age. And I mean something valid."

Raleigh chuckled. "You know, Valentine, I have a strange feeling that you don't trust many people. Or is it only men you don't trust?" he asked softly, suspecting that was the truth, and knowing he was prying too deeply too soon.

She looked away briefly, then returned his smile. "It's only you," she said flippantly. "I've never known such a cosmopolitan man—a great writer, a world traveler. I wouldn't put it past you at all to fib to me just to get your way."

Raleigh wanted his way with her all right, but he had no intention in the world of fibbing to her. He wanted her to trust him. It was too early to know what the future held for either of them, but he was going to be on the level with her as much as possible.

"I don't need to lie to you, Valentine," he said seriously. "And I won't."

Their gazes held; Valentine had the feeling that he was implying a lot more than he was saying. She didn't know why it made her so nervous.

Abruptly, he removed his wallet and showed her so much identification that she laughed aloud. "All right! All right! I lose! I'll make the cake," she said.

"And you'll tell me how damned good I look for thirty-six, won't you?" he teased. "Obviously I had you fooled."

He had expressed one of Valentine's most blatant worries: that he *was* trying to fool her. That he would make a fool of her. That she would be his laugh while he was in town. She was afraid he could accomplish that with the greatest of ease, if she weren't on her guard. And she hadn't been, for most of the time in the restaurant.

"Yes, I'll admit you fooled me," she said. "But only by one year. After all I did guess that you were no more than thirty-five."

"With prompting," he joked. "You began by thinking I was a lot younger."

"I did," she said.

They both seemed surprised when their food arrived. They had barely made a dent in the antipasto tray and their wineglasses were only a third empty.

"See," Raleigh said, "dinner didn't stand in the way of our catering discussion after all. In fact, it seems we've pretty much ignored dinner. Let's eat. What do you say?"

Valentine smiled. "I say fine."

She wanted to forget about baking him a birthday cake, at least for now. It was just one more connection to him, but she'd made the bet, and of course she would stand by it.

Anyway, she realized that she was hungry after all. Somehow she had forgotten all about Brady and the fact that she and Raleigh were having a meal she and her former fiancé always shared.

"It looks divine," she added.

So did she, Raleigh thought to himself. He took another drink of his wine, then began to eat the pasta. Perhaps, he reasoned, if he were sated enough from the meal, he wouldn't think so much about this pretty woman across from him. Perhaps.

* * *

It didn't work. An hour later, after he and Valentine had shared another brief chat with Maria and Genna and had complimented the older woman on her cooking, Raleigh couldn't wait to escort Valentine to the car. He wanted to be completely alone with her more than anything he'd wanted in a long, long time.

Valentine, too relaxed from the wine and rich food, found herself smiling as Raleigh helped her into the car. She liked this debonair, sophisticated man. She liked him a lot. And therein lay the danger.

"We really are going for a moonlight ride," he told her when he'd started the car.

Valentine laughed. "Raleigh, I hate to tell you, but there is no moon." She bent forward so she could gaze out the car window. "It looks like rain, if I'm any judge of the weather."

He grinned. "All the better."

"Why?" she asked innocently.

Looking at her, Raleigh tried to decide if he should tell her how irresistible he found her tonight. Good sense prevailed.

"I love the rain," he said honestly. "Do you?"

Valentine shrugged a little. In truth, she did. She found the patter of rain very soothing, very mesmerizing. Especially the soft southern rains that came in spring. She even liked the storms with their hard, driving rains, their winds, their thunder and lightning.

"Is that a yes or no?" Raleigh persisted.

"I like the rain," she confessed. And I like you. Too much, she added mentally.

"It can be very romantic, can't it?" he murmured.

Valentine wondered if it was her imagination, or did

Raleigh keep mentioning romance? And why? Was it his nature? Was it her? Was it the night?

She swiftly wiped the forming thoughts from her mind. She wasn't silly enough to let this man take her for a ride. As she had predicted, a gentle rain had begun to fall. The sound of the faint drops on the car's roof were almost hypnotic.

"I really think you'd better take me home," she said, the tone that Raleigh was beginning to despise returning to her voice.

"Just a short ride," he said, trying to soften her up a little. He wanted to spend more time with her.

"Raleigh!" she protested. "We have a twenty-five-mile ride home as it is. How can you take a *short* ride anywhere?"

He chuckled. "I want to take you to a spot up on a hill where we can see all of the town. It's really very pretty," he said.

"No," she said firmly. She had no doubt that he had a pretty spot in mind—pretty and romantic—and she had better sense than to go with him. "We came to discuss business, and we've done that. I really must get home. The ride will be long enough."

He'd already pulled out into the street, but that didn't stop him from laying one hand on the back of the seat right behind Valentine's head. She tensed as she felt his fingers caress her neck.

"Are you sure?" he asked. "The view from the top of the hill is something special."

If she hadn't been sure before, she certainly was now. "Positive."

Raleigh wanted to protest, to insist. He wanted to

swear and complain. He had intended to hold her there on that hill.

But he knew it wouldn't do any good to press her. He could only thank his lucky stars that he would be seeing her again on catering business, and that she was now obligated to bake him a birthday cake. He decided at that moment that he wanted a party, too—just for him and her.

"Well," he said, trying not to let the disappointment and resentment he felt creep into his voice, "I guess you mean business when you say business, lady."

Valentine recalled how he'd told Genna and Maria that she was his lady. She wasn't, of course. There was no point in pretending. She wasn't ready for more heartache, and she wasn't about to be his means of keeping boredom at bay while he was in town—no matter how appealing the idea of spending time with him was to her.

Although she didn't see his jaw muscles clench in frustration, she was aware that he was very silent on the return trip.

When he had parked the car in front of her cottage, he asked, "When can we discuss the wedding again? Carolyn is going to give me the approximate guest count, so we can judge how much food we'll need."

Forcing a bright smile, Valentine said, "Come into the shop anytime. I'm open from six to five. I'm there most of the time."

Damn, Raleigh swore silently to himself. She was a hard woman to win over. He'd thought he was making progress at dinner; now he felt that he was losing ground again. He got out of the car and went around to her side. Valentine had already gotten out.

"I'll see you to the door," Raleigh insisted.

"Really, that won't be necessary. It's raining. Please get back in the car."

"It might not be necessary," he said, trying to keep his tone light, "but I like the rain, remember, and I'd like to walk you to the door. May I do that?"

What could she say? "Yes, if you aren't afraid you'll melt," she said, trying to make a joke of it.

"I'm more afraid that you will," he said. He really did have an overwhelming urge to protect this woman. Despite her being a businesswoman who was obviously doing well with her ambitions, she seemed fragile in a way he'd never known; it touched something deep within him.

"I won't melt," she said. "Apparently I'm tougher than you think."

Raleigh laughed gently, but he doubted that it was so.

Once again Valentine was much too aware of his presence as she went up the cobbled walk with him. Fortunately for her, he didn't try to hold her hand or tuck her arm beneath his.

"Good night," she said when they reached her front porch.

"Aren't you even going to let me come in out of the rain?" he asked softly.

She shook her head; she had better sense than to invite him in. "You like the rain, remember?"

"Touché!" he said, trying to inject some laughter into the word. He stood awkwardly on the porch for a moment, knowing how badly he wanted to hold her, to feel her body against his.

"Good night," she repeated, turning to insert her door key.

"Good night," he murmured.

Valentine looked back over her shoulder to give him a parting smile, and unexpectedly, he drew her up against his body, his lips easily claiming hers in a passionate kiss. Her mouth was sweet, so very, very sweet and pliable. She didn't try to resist, and Raleigh sighed in satisfaction. He could feel his heart beating as rapidly as a young boy's; the adrenaline was surging through him like nothing he'd ever known, and he'd been in many situations that had caused his heart to race.

He was aware of Valentine's soft sigh of surrender as her tongue met his in the secret darkness of their mouths. He molded her more tightly to his body, grateful that she wore heels. Each slender curve fit as perfectly against him as he had suspected it would.

His mouth moved against hers more possessively and, to his pleasure, Valentine met the heat in his kiss. Although he had known she would be passionate, she was even more exciting than he had imagined. Her hunger was equal to his own, and that was saying something.

Valentine moaned again. The reality of Raleigh's loving was even more potent than she had thought possible. She had been so determined to resist him, but something about him called out to the woman in her. It seemed as natural to be in his arms as it did to breathe.

His mouth strayed from hers to kiss her neck and Valentine automatically arched it to give him easier access. His long fingers sought her breasts, teasing the peaks unmercifully, causing Valentine to suck in her breath at the thrill that shot through her.

She wanted to press closer and closer to him, to feel his fire and his desire. There was no doubt that he wanted her. She was aware of his growing response.

Suddenly, she snapped out of her love-induced stupor. Good Lord! What on earth was she doing?

When—and if—she ever allowed herself to become involved with another man, she didn't want it to be like this, in a mad rush of passion with a stranger who quickly came into her life and would just as quickly leave it.

"Stop," she whispered, half pleading as she forced herself free of his possessive embrace. She knew she was as much to blame for this situation as he was.

"Valentine, oh, sweet Valentine," Raleigh murmured in a passion-thick voice, "don't do this to me."

"I—I'm sorry," she murmured tremulously. This had gotten out of hand so fast that she hadn't even known what was happening.

"Don't run away like this—not now," Raleigh said hoarsely.

But Valentine had already managed to get free of his embrace; she escaped while she still could. Her legs trembling, her whole body quivering, she opened the door, entered the sanctuary of her house, and quickly shut Raleigh out.

For a long time he stood on the porch, trying to pull himself together. Breathing raggedly, his heart hammering, the scent and touch of Valentine still lingering, he tried to compose himself to return to his sister's house.

He'd gone about this all wrong, he chastised himself. Valentine Smith wasn't the kind of woman a man persuaded to discuss business over dinner, then tried to ravish at her door.

But then, he hadn't expected things to go as far as they had. He simply hadn't been able to resist kissing her. And once he'd done that and she'd responded—

A fever raced through him. He was burning up. Abruptly, he stepped off the porch into the misty rain. As if on cue, the skies opened up and began to pour. Raleigh welcomed the cloudburst. He needed something to cool him down.

Inside the house, Valentine went to the window and peeked out. Feeling wretched and guilty, she watched as Raleigh walked to his car in the pouring rain. She was almost tempted to run out and tell him to come in until the worst of it was over.

Almost. She knew what would happen if he came near her again. She was still on fire from his caresses. She had to have some time to get herself together. Lord, she felt ashamed of the way she had fallen into his arms. She had wanted him, really wanted him, as she had never wanted another man.

She hoped by some miracle that he would decide to give the job of catering consultant back to Carolyn. Otherwise she didn't know what she would do. She didn't see how she could ever face him again. She was embarrassed and feeling humiliated once more.

But worse—much worse—she longed to be back in Raleigh Coseegan's arms!

CHAPTER SIX

VALENTINE THREW HERSELF into her work, doing her best to forget Raleigh and the evening they had shared. But, try as she might, she couldn't forget his kisses or the way he'd felt against her body. It was as though she'd been on fire since.

Each morning when she went to work, she was tense, waiting for him to pop into the shop. Three days passed, and there was no sign of him. Then, just when she was beginning to relax again, to let her guard down, she looked up to see him enter the building.

Immediately, her heart began to pound and she felt breathless. Dressed in form-fitting jeans and a blue pull-over shirt, he was more devastatingly handsome than usual.

Or did Valentine only think so because in her heart she had ached to see him again? The suspense had been killing her. She'd told herself that she wanted Carolyn to take over as catering consultant, yet she had been afraid that was exactly what would happen and she wouldn't see Raleigh again until the wedding. If then—

His eyes caught hers, and she brushed at the dough that still clung to her hands. "Good morning," he said warmly, as if they were friendly strangers, as if he hadn't almost made love to her on her porch a few short nights ago.

"Good morning." She hoped the breathless way she felt wasn't apparent in her voice.

Lucy, who had been taking brownies off a tray, poked her head around to see who had entered the shop.

"Oh, good morning, Mr. Coseegan!" she said cheerily. She turned to Valentine. "Shall I see to him, miss?"

Valentine longed to say yes, but she wanted to talk to him too badly herself. "He's probably here about the wedding," she said in a low voice. "I'll take care of it."

"Fine," Lucy said agreeably as she went back to the brownies. Just as Valentine took off her apron and smoothed down her slacks and shirt, Lucy looked back out from the kitchen. "We've got nice hot delicious brownies here, Mr. Coseegan, that Miss Smith just baked. I'm just taking them up this minute. You might like a couple."

He grinned. "I believe I might, Lucy," he said warmly, but his eyes were only for Valentine. She wished that he seemed even a little bit uncomfortable— *she* was falling apart—but he was apparently as confident and calm as ever.

"I would like a couple of brownies and a cup of coffee, if that's okay," he said. "I've got the guest list. Do you have a few minutes to talk about the wedding?"

Oh, Lord, Valentine thought to herself, he was really going to go through with this. Didn't he know how he caused her stomach to flipflop? Didn't he know the sensual effect he had on her? Couldn't he tell how attracted she was to him? Was he going to take her at her word and stick to business? She didn't think she could stand it.

"Fine," she said in a voice that didn't even sound like her own. "I'll get coffee and brownies for both of us. I need a breather anyway."

Raleigh tried to act nonchalant as he watched her walk away, but suddenly he was feeling like a little boy. He was daydreaming about how much he would love to take this woman to his bed and kiss her until they both were heady with the sensations of lovemaking. He wanted to stroke her silky skin until she trembled with desire. He ached to feel her hips moving rhythmically beneath his.

He seemed actually startled when she turned around with two cups of coffee in hand; he tried his best to remember that he was here under the excuse of wedding business.

"Mmm, that smells good," he said. "I haven't had my first cup yet this morning and I love to start the day with hot coffee."

"Neither have I," Valentine said as she set the cups down with barely steady fingers. How was she going to get through this? She'd rather start the morning with one of his kisses than a thousand cups of hot coffee.

"I'll be right back with the brownies," she said, grateful for an excuse to rush away again. In the kitchen, she drew in several steadying breaths. Lucy, seeing that Valentine looked paler than usual, put a motherly hand on her shoulder.

"Miss Smith, what's wrong, honey?"

Valentine shook her head. "Nothing, really, Lucy." Nothing but weak legs and upside-down stomach. Nothing but shivers up and down her spine. Nothing but Raleigh Coseegan.

She smiled at the older woman and forced herself to say something else. "I do wish you would call me Valentine."

Lucy stubbornly shook her head. "Ain't at all proper to be calling the boss by her first name, even such a young one as you."

She patted Valentine on the shoulder again. "Course, I suppose I shouldn't be patting on you either, but, child, I'm always feeling like you're needing someone."

Lucy's brown eyes were expressive with emotion. "I'm real proud of you, honey, as if you were one of my own. I just want you to know old Lucy's here for you if you need me."

Valentine could feel tears welling in her blue eyes. Something about Lucy's concern and gentle manner reminded her of her grandfather. How she missed him and his practical advice at times like this!

She wondered if Lucy had any idea what her problem really was, if she could tell that the mere presence of Raleigh Coseegan made her quiver all over and lose what little sense she had left after his near-seduction the other night.

She drew in another breath and briefly closed her eyes. "Thank you, Lucy. You've gone out of your way to be kind and helpful. It means more to me than I can tell you, but I'll be all right."

"Is it that nasty old Mr. Carruthers?" Lucy asked in a low voice. "Has he been pestering you at home again?"

Relieved because Lucy had totally misread the situation, Valentine suddenly laughed aloud. "He's been calling," she confessed, the laughter easing some of the tension she was feeling. "Thank God, the money I—" Her words trailed off.

Stars above! She'd almost told Lucy she'd earned money belly dancing! Truly she was no good at lies and deception. "The money I managed to scrape together will hold him at bay another month. Then it looks like the Domini-Duncan wedding will be our salvation."

She glanced back out at Raleigh, who was looking in her direction. In a quiet voice she murmured to Lucy, "Mr. Coseegan said spare no expense. They really want this wedding to be a memorable and extravagant occasion."

"Good!" Lucy whispered excitedly. "Good! Well, you get on out there and take care of him."

Take care of him, Valentine repeated to herself. She was sure he could handle her, yet she had no idea on earth what to do with him.

She smiled to herself. Lucy, of course, was talking about business. Thank heavens, she didn't know that Raleigh had Valentine all in knots and barely in control.

She nodded, took three of the largest and most delectable-looking brownies, and returned to the table where Raleigh sat.

"I heard you laughing," he said. "You have such a great laugh. You should do it more often."

Valentine met his eyes. Here we go again with the compliments, she told herself. The man was just so darned irresistible; even though she tried to tell herself that flattery was second nature to him, she clung eagerly to every kind word. It was nice to hear something besides thief, embezzler, and worse things that she kept trying to forget.

"I laugh," she said casually, "when I have something to laugh about." She met his eyes again. In truth, she had found more things to laugh about recently than she had in a long, long time; still, she was afraid of letting herself be natural with Raleigh, afraid of winding up as his joke.

She honestly didn't think she could bear it so soon after Brady and the threat of the trial she'd lived through. She shivered internally. The shame, the humiliation, had almost been her undoing, truly it had.

Abruptly, Raleigh reached over and took her hand when she set the brownies down. "I'd like to be the one to make you laugh, Valentine," he said.

Jerking her hand away as if he had burned her, Valentine quickly glanced around at her other customers. Puzzled, feeling more than a little rejected and at a loss to understand whether this woman was just embarrassed or simply didn't want him around, Raleigh immediately clenched his hands into fists.

Damn, she had him in knots. She was so hard on his ego that he was beginning to feel like a high school kid again. If she hadn't come to him eagerly, hungrily when he kissed her the other night; he'd really think she wasn't at all interested.

He shook his head. It wasn't like him to be daunted

by a woman. He had more confidence than that, a hell of a lot more. He'd been with enough women to know when one was interested. It was just that this one was so wary. He seemed always to be breeching some code of ethics Valentine Smith had. Clearly she didn't want anyone to see him courting her in the shop.

He laughed at the archaic expression: courting. Yet that was exactly what he felt like he had to do with this woman, with this reluctant southern belle who was so wary of his advances, yet so wildly passionate in his arms. He really didn't understand her reluctance.

Instinctively, he knew that she wasn't the coy type. She really wasn't trying to play a game with him. After all, he was the one who was pressing.

In truth, he supposed the challenge was beginning to spur him. He'd always been tenacious to a fault, and he wasn't about to let something he wanted as badly as Valentine put him off course.

"Sorry," he murmured. "I'm afraid I can't seem to keep my hands off you. Please don't drive me from the shop with stones and harsh words."

Valentine couldn't keep from smiling at the image of her chasing Raleigh Coseegan from her shop—period —much less with stones and harsh words.

"I believe you were going to bring in the guest list," she said, trying her best to adopt a businesslike demeanor.

"Only if you'll smile again for me," he said, furiously trying to divert the crisp professional image she was dredging up. "Come on, admit it. I amused you, didn't I? I touched your funny bone with my stones-and-harsh-words comment."

Shaking her head, Valentine had to smile again. "Raleigh, I'm afraid you're incorrigible."

"Me!" he said, pretending shock. "Raleigh Coseegan? Not me, of all men! In fact, that sounds downright dangerous!"

"Yes, you," she said, still fighting a smile. "You can't do business with a woman—any woman—without trying to woo her." And that was dangerous, she acknowledged to herself. Very dangerous for the unwary.

"*Woo*, her," he murmured. "My God, that does sound exciting! What are the chances in this case? Are you up to some wooing? I am if you are," he said with a wide grin.

Valentine stared at him for a long moment, then reached for her coffee with trembling hands. After she drank a bit of the steaming brew, which warmed and soothed her insides, she looked into Raleigh's dark eyes again. No, she wasn't up to being wooed by this man, not a little, not at all. She was too scared.

"The guest list?" she prompted. "You do have it, don't you?"

With surprise, Raleigh realized that his hands were unsteady when he withdrew the list from his pocket. He suddenly felt on shaky ground. He wanted to get to know this woman so badly, and the more she ran hot and cold on him, the more frantic he felt. Minutes ago he'd been sure she was thawing, but now that cold, professional tone was back again. Dammit! She was frustrating!

He was only going to be here for a short time. There was no way on earth that he could get out of his next assignment. What he wrote could very well influence, or at least embarrass, a foreign government so that it would release a political prisoner, a prisoner who needed desperately to be freed before age and illness ended his life. It was all very top secret.

While Raleigh hoped he could convince himself that this really would be the last assignment he would take, he'd said the same thing about the last one. This one was an assignment he just couldn't turn down.

That was before Valentine Smith, it was true, but this line of work wasn't for a married man. *Married?* He didn't know why the very word unsettled him so. He knew he'd been thinking about it ever since he'd met Valentine, but it was too soon.

What about this elusive Valentine Smith he'd met so suddenly and unexpectedly? Could he win her over in the brief time he had left before the assignment? Was that even fair? He was in turmoil over this woman, and he couldn't afford to lose his head, not even for a moment. He'd always been a man who kept his cool, no matter what—until Valentine.

The situation was precarious. He needed to make headway while she was vulnerable and opening up, no matter how slightly. She wasn't a woman to be rushed, obviously. He had seen her passion and her spirit, but he had also seen her guardedness. He had to proceed cautiously to have any hope of capturing her heart, and yet he knew instinctively that if he didn't keep up the pursuit somehow, he would lose her.

He truly feared that if he went to the Middle East for a few weeks, Valentine Smith would be lost to him forever. But he couldn't tell her about his next mission.

And he knew, sitting across from her in this sunny little small-town bakery, that it mattered very much to him. It might even matter to his entire future. That scared him.

What if marriage wasn't for him? What if he told her he had to be away awhile on an assignment, but that he had every intention of coming back for her? He was almost positive she'd been hurt by a man at some time. Damn! He hated this indecisiveness in himself. It was just another sign that he should indeed get out of the business. Hell, he didn't even want to think about it anymore. Maybe he'd know more by the time he had to leave.

"Here's the list," he said, managing another smile. "It's a humdinger."

And that it was! Valentine stared at it in shock. There was an open church to the ceremony, and an open invitation to everyone who patronized the restaurant, in addition to the regular guest list of family and close friends.

"Raleigh, are you serious?" she gasped. "Good heavens, I'll need to start baking right away if this list is for real. The last I heard, about two hundred people were expected!"

He wanted to reach for her hand again, but resisted. "You can handle it," he said calmly. "Carolyn, Tod, and I discussed it last night. Now originally, it's true, we were going to invite select people; however, it's become Carolyn's big dream to show the townspeople how much she appreciates their patronage."

When he saw that the stunned look was still in her eyes, he continued quickly. "I know it's a little unusual, but now we've decided to expand the invitation to more townspeople. After all, we're holding the wedding in the park. I understand it will accommodate the people who want to come. Not everyone will attend of course."

"No, of course not," Valentine said, trying to digest what he was saying. "Regardless, Raleigh, there are *eleven thousand* people in this town, give or take a few. A whole lot of them *will* come. The restaurant is the most popular for miles around."

He grinned. "Well, eleven thousand won't come, of course, but we certainly hope a few hundred will. What's the point in inviting them if they don't?"

She shook her head. "This isn't a laughing matter." Her alarmed blue eyes searched his. "I'm honored and I'm flattered, and I'm pleased your family has enough confidence in me to think I can do this, but mine is a small bakery. Of course I could hire some additional temporary help, but still—"

This time Raleigh couldn't resist taking her hands in his. "Listen to me, Valentine. I know this is a big order, but we're all going to work with you on it. Two of the ladies' auxiliaries and a couple of the women's clubs are going to bring cookies and punch. To my sister's delight, much of the town seems to be thrilled about the occasion. And, after all, it's a bright new season and a fun thing to do. Romance is always popular."

"Raleigh, *still*—"

She hadn't even realized that he was holding her hands, much less that she was hanging on for dear life. This wedding was way out of her league, just like this man. She was going to make an utter fool of herself. She couldn't carry this off.

"Val," he said soothingly, "Carolyn and Tod will prepare some of the food at the restaurant, and Maria is simply insistent that she get to cook some of the desserts. One of the soft drink dealers wants to contribute beverages. Now if you'll just settle down, we'll all pull together on this, and it'll be magical. You'll see. It may sound like a circus at this point, but, truly, I've attended weddings where there were more guests than even live in this town. It honestly can be a wondrous and memorable wedding—the proverbial fairy-tale wedding, if you will."

She believed him. Looking into his dark, calming eyes, Valentine felt her heartbeat slow. Her hands began to stop shaking, and when she loosened her grip, she was aghast to look down and see that she had been clutching Raleigh's hands tightly.

"I'm sorry!" she cried, quickly snatching her hands back.

He grinned. "I'm not. I like you holding on to me. I like it a lot."

She could feel her heart flutter. She liked holding on to him, too, and she didn't want to. She couldn't let herself.

"Raleigh," she murmured, trying frantically to compose her thoughts and the turmoil in her mind, "I haven't been in the bakery business long. This is a fantastic opportunity for me. I want very much to do it right."

She looked levelly into his dark eyes. "I appreciate your concern and your willingness to help me with this, but I do not"—she hesitated, because she knew she was about to tell a monumental lie—"I do not want, or welcome, your personal interest in me. I've tried to make you understand from the beginning that this is business. It *has* to be business."

Stung once again by her rejection, yet feeling that he didn't really have the right to be so personally insulted when she had made her position plain from the start, Raleigh spoke sharply. "I understand perfectly, lady!"

He ran both hands through his curly dark blond hair in a gesture of total frustration.

For the first time, Valentine noticed the thin scar on his beautifully shaped mouth. In his undisguised anger, it seemed to stand out whitely from his lips.

"Raleigh—" she whispered, not even sure what she wanted to say.

He sighed heavily. It was on the tip of his tongue to tell her that he knew that she was Angelina the belly dancer and that he still understood "no" as well as he had that first night.

However, he didn't believe she meant no now. A woman couldn't have kissed him as this one had and still *really* mean no. She might wish she did, and in fact, he felt sure she did wish it, but he was certain the odds were on his side if he could just keep his temper and bide his time.

Only God knew how hard that was for a man like him, bold, rash, reckless, used to getting what he wanted, no matter what that took. However, Valentine Smith wasn't a story or an interview. Or a woman actively manhunting.

She was a vulnerable woman, whatever the reasons: fear of not being able to make a success of her business; fear of involvement with a man for her own reasons;

fear from the past. He didn't know. He just knew she was driving him insane.

He drew in a steadying breath and looked directly into her blue eyes. In a blinding flash, it finally occurred to him that maybe she believed he was trying to force his attentions on her under the guise of helping with the wedding, and that was what was galling her. After all, he would be no better than old man Carruthers, who'd raised her rent in an attempt at getting her to go out with him.

"Valentine, you and I both know that I find you very attractive," he admitted frankly. "I am not going to play games with you or mislead you. I did volunteer to help Carolyn with this wedding, not only because she needed help—the affair keeps mushrooming—but because I wanted to get to know you. The first time I saw you, I knew I wanted to get to know you."

Valentine looked away and hoped he didn't notice the blush on her cheeks. The first time he'd seen her, she'd been on stage, and he'd laughed at her. Is that what he was referring to? He continued talking before she could sort out the confusion in her mind and decide what to say.

"I believe I made that obvious right from the start. I insisted on dinner because I wanted to see you outside the workplace; however, I'm not trying to interfere with your business, and I'm not putting pressure on you to become personally involved with me if that's something you really don't want."

He paused to study her face. "The wedding has nothing to do with that. The job is, and has been, yours, no matter what happens between you and me. Maybe I am out of line here. Maybe I am a vain fool, yet when you returned my kiss, I thought you felt some attraction for me, too."

Valentine stared down at her cooling coffee. She was unreasonably grateful to him for being honest and open with her. As scared as she was of being equally honest with him, she did feel that he deserved the truth—at least about the bank and her position in town. He hadn't mentioned knowing that she was Angelina, and she couldn't bring herself to either. One confession at a time was hard enough for her.

Never allowing her gaze to leave her coffee cup, feeling her face turn redder and redder, she told Raleigh what had happened to her with Brady and the bank, and how afraid she was of scandal, how much this job meant to her. Then she looked up at him.

"I am attracted to you, it's true, but I will not let myself be your distraction while you're in this small town, then become a memory for you while the town gossips. I couldn't stand it."

Raleigh felt his insides tighten. He wanted to kill this Brady for hurting her, but he was suddenly at a loss for words, too. He didn't know how truthful to be with her, because he wasn't sure himself what his future held. He traced the rim of his coffee cup.

"I want to get as much of this out in the open as I can," he told her finally. "Number one, I happen to like this town. Now, granted, it's a new notion to me. I've grown weary of war and broken countries and lives. I'm seriously considering settling down and fictionalizing some of my experiences, or maybe even doing travel books. This little town seems very conducive to that idea."

He looked away in thought. "I don't know that I *can* settle down," he said frankly. "I've been a roustabout and a rover all my life."

He looked back at her. "But I'm exploring my possibilities, especially since I met you, Valentine. I swear that's not a lie. You—your beauty, your frankness, your freshness, even your vulnerability and your determination to make a go of your business—strike a chord in me, touch some part of me that no woman has before."

"Raleigh—" Valentine said, suddenly needing very much to tell him her part in the belly-dance deception.

He silenced her with his fingertip against her lips. "Please don't condemn me on the basis of your past. I think we might have something good here. Can't we at least start as friends?"

Chewing on her lip, Valentine reflected upon what he'd said. She was suddenly awash with turmoil and fear. Some part of her wished he hadn't said any of it. He had come into her life at a time when she needed someone to care—needed someone to make her feel like a woman again. She hadn't allowed herself to think about that, to realize what Brady had done not only to her reputation, but to her sense of self, until Raleigh started giving her so much attention.

But was he the someone she needed? And could he settle down? She was afraid; instinctively, she trusted that he was telling her the truth as he saw it. But he was blunt about his own doubts. Could she afford to trust herself or him on this? To involve her heart and ego with such a man?

She looked into his dark eyes and she knew she wanted to trust herself. She wanted to trust him. She wanted—she wanted—she didn't even know what. Some miracle maybe, to make this all work out right for them.

Heaven help her, she was more than attracted to Raleigh Coseegan. She had known him less than a week, and she knew she could fall for him as she never had for another man. How could she refuse his request that they at least start as friends? How on earth, when her heart was begging her to say yes?

Feeling as though she was taking a big, big step, she nodded. "Friends," she said at last, wondering at the very word itself. "But as you pointed out, I'm rather like one of those traditional southern belles. Please don't rush me." The plea was, of course, just another attempt at protecting herself from the pain of love that could come from this man.

Raleigh wanted to heave a huge sigh of relief. He felt ridiculous coaxing this woman to accept his attentions, no matter what term they used.

Oh, he wanted to be friends with her all right. He believed that was an important part of the relationship between a man and a woman, but God knew he wanted more, a lot more than friendship. So much more that it undermined him. Along with his bold and reckless nature, he had inherited a natural predisposition for cunningly assessing a situation and instinctively handling it to his advantage. It was almost like a sixth sense with him.

But Valentine Smith wasn't a situation, either. There was no way to analyze her, to assess their relationship

—or lack of one—to methodically plot it to the conclusion he wanted. He didn't know how to deal with this.

"Thanks," he finally said, casually, making himself smile at her. His heart was beating hard, and he felt as though he'd survived the crossing of some barrier. "You won't be sorry," he said with a bold wink. "I'm not such bad company, really I'm not."

"I know," she said a little softly.

That was an incredible understatement. He was intriguing company. He was *fascinating* company. He was an unusual and amazing man.

"I promise you here and now, Valentine Smith," he said very earnestly, "that you won't regret your decision. I will never make you sorry that you agreed, and believe me when I tell you that you aren't a distraction for me while I'm here."

He laughed. "I'd better rephrase that. You *are* a distraction, no doubt about it. I don't think I've ever been so distracted by a woman, or worked so hard in my life pursuing her, but you're not just fun and games for me for the time I'll be here. I promise you that."

A smile trembled on Valentine's lips. A moment ago she'd thought she'd done the right thing by agreeing to be Raleigh's friend; now she wasn't so sure. He'd said all the right things to reassure her that she meant something to him more than just someone to occupy time.

But somehow all his reassurances caused fresh doubts to surge into her mind. Was he attracted because he found her elusive? Was she only a challenge to a man unused to being thwarted in his desires? She was just an ordinary woman. Why was he so interested?

Most of all, she couldn't forget that he said she

wouldn't be just fun and games for him. She couldn't forget that when he'd stood outside the dressing room door the night of the belly dance, he'd said he took his laughs where he could find them. She had a sudden compulsion to tell him that she had been Angelina.

She couldn't make herself do it. If they were clearing the air, as they appeared to be, and he knew she was Angelina, why hadn't he said so? She'd already bared her soul much more than she'd ever intended.

She shifted in her chair and looked down at the guest list. She was feeling insecure again. And it wasn't just because of the incredible number of invitees.

She gazed across at the handsome, smiling blond man. Her insecurity came from Raleigh Coseegan himself. She knew in her heart that he had the power to hurt her as Brady never had.

It was a scary feeling. Scary and heady at the same time.

CHAPTER SEVEN

"NOW, I REALIZE that you don't know this area much better than I," Raleigh said, "but I need a favor already, friend."

Her eyes widened as her gaze met his. "What?"

He chuckled. "Don't look as though I'm asking you to lay your head on the chopping block, Valentine."

She managed a smile. She really felt as though she'd already lain her head there. "What's the favor?"

"I want to give Randolph and Mimmi a house for their wedding gift. I know that Randolph is crazy about a place called Smith Mountain Lake."

Valentine swallowed and wondered if she should tell Raleigh how expensive the lake area was. She didn't know what his finances were, of course, but then he had said money was no object in the wedding expenses. She decided not to mention the cost of living at the lake.

"I've only been there one time myself," she said. She grinned. "But I can read a map, and so can a world traveler like you."

He laughed. "Getting there really isn't the problem. I need a woman's touch. Would you believe that I have never purchased a house in my life? My home base has always been New York, where I keep an apartment that I just stumbled onto and have lived there ever since. Most of my time is spent in hotels and on planes and trains and in rental cars."

"Poor baby," she teased. "What a miserable existence for you."

He laughed. "Actually it can be. You have no idea what jet lag can do to a body unless you've traveled that much. Despite looking so young," he joked, "gravity has taken its toll on this body."

Valentine couldn't help thinking every other body should be so lucky as to look like Raleigh's after gravity had taken its toll. Lord, he was attractive.

"What do you say?" he asked. "Will you ride up there with me tomorrow when you finish up here?"

Valentine realized that she'd forgotten the question; she'd been so busy staring at him.

"What? Oh, the house—yes," she answered quickly. "I'll go with you to look at houses, although I assure you, I'm no house expert myself. My cottage is the only place I've ever bought, and I picked it partly because it was so close to the shop."

"From what little I saw of it," he said, "I found it very homey and attractive. I think that's the kind of place Randolph and Mimmi would be comfortable in. Again," he said, relieving her of the burden about introducing house costs at the lake, "money really isn't a problem."

He laughed. "Not that I'd want you to think I'm rich —I'm not, and I don't want you chasing me for my money—"

Instantly indignant, Valentine shot back at him, "You have an incredibly arrogant opinion of yourself! I'm not chasing you at all, Mr. Coseegan, and believe me, your money or lack of it is no concern of mine! I make my own way in this world!"

He grinned and slowly shook his head. "My, my, you're a feisty, independent little thing when you want to be, aren't you? What a temper! I promise I was only teasing."

"You promise too much," she retorted, still not placated. She didn't know what she was angrier about, that he suggested *she* was chasing *him* or that he suggested she was after anybody's *money*. God, after that embezzling business, she didn't want to touch a dime that wasn't her own, even in the line of work!

"Oh?" He murmured, still trying to calm her down. "How about you promising a thing or two? How about promising that you won't ever, ever call me Mr. Coseegan again, and how about working at not being so defensive about money." He winked. "I do love a woman with a temper and spirit, but not when they're directed at me without cause."

Valentine sighed. "I'm sure you simply love women —period—Raleigh. Still, I'll try not to overreact."

"Now wait a minute," he murmured, smiling broadly. "I didn't say I wanted you never to overreact." He reached for her hand. "Confidentially, lady, the way you responded to my kisses the other night was thrilling."

"Raleigh," she cautioned, her face reddening as she glanced around, suddenly remembering her other customers, "we're starting as friends, remember?"

"I remember," he whispered, "but there are some things a man can't forget and your kisses are one of them."

Abruptly, Valentine stood up, snatched up the guest list and stuffed it into her apron pocket. "I've got to get busy. I hadn't realized so many people had come in, and I'm still baking."

Raleigh grabbed her hand before she could escape. "Tomorrow night here at five," he said.

She nodded, then rushed back to the kitchen. She waited until Raleigh had had time to leave, then she watched him walk down the street. A smile brightened her entire face. He had loved her kisses!

Still smiling, she went back out to clean off the table they had vacated. Neither one of them had had more than a few swallows of coffee, and the brownies were virtually untouched.

Raleigh had left a five-dollar bill on the table. Valentine picked it up. She would return it to him tomorrow night and tease him about not liking her brownies.

Valentine thought the day would never end. Foolishly, she kept smiling to herself, thinking over the things Raleigh had said to her. She was frightened, but she was flattered by his interest. She was looking forward to going with him to Smith Mountain Lake far more than she should have been.

Every time she and Lucy talked abut the preparations for the phenomenal wedding, which was to occur much too soon, Valentine became more and more excited. Her mind was filled with ideas to make the exceptional occasion a most memorable one, not only for the bride and groom, but for the town and herself as well. The more she thought about it, the more of an honor she felt it was that she had been selected to cater this fantastic event.

And the more she thought about Raleigh Coseegan.

Five o'clock the next day arrived almost before she knew it. Valentine had brought along a change of clothing, jeans and a clean shirt. She wished she'd told Raleigh to pick her up at her house instead of at the shop. She wanted to shower and freshen up.

She had put her hair in a braid for work, and even though she had brushed it until it flowed down her back in waves, she wasn't happy with it. She suddenly found herself wishing she were beautiful and sophisticated like the other women who surely must populate Raleigh's life.

She shook her head. What was the point in wishing? She was who she was and, generally, now that the awful time of Brady was behind her, she was very happy with herself. She loved the shop more than she had ever thought possible; she had been fortunate in choosing this town to make a new start. She really was doing very well.

She jumped when the bell over the front door rang. She had locked the door promptly at five so that she could come back to the restroom and get ready for Raleigh without late customers coming in. Lucy had al-

ready gone home. Raleigh was, no doubt, the one ring-
ing the bell.

With one final glance in the mirror, she turned away.
Her pulse was racing by the time she got to the front of
the store. Raleigh was on the other side of the multi-
paned door, smiling at her. Valentine wanted to stand
opposite him for just a moment, with the door as a barrier, until she could catch her breath.

She was always amazed by his good looks, no matter
how many times she saw him. Today he was in tight,
faded jeans that fit his body like a second skin. A
tucked-in navy shirt accentuated his muscled chest and
slim waist. He wore boots, which made him look even
more masculine than usual. Valentine's heart was doing
incredibly crazy things inside her chest as she stared at
him.

He motioned for her to unlock the door, and she
laughed nervously. She really was losing her mind,
standing there staring at him like a starstruck fool.

"I'm sorry," she said, still smiling nervously as she
opened the door for him.

"You must have forgotten it was locked," he said,
giving her just the excuse she needed for behaving foolishly.

She nodded. "I was in the bathroom changing. I
didn't think you'd want me to wear my work clothes."

He smiled. "I'm sure anything you wear would suit
me just fine, but I'm glad you're in jeans." His eyes
roved boldly over her in a way she was becoming used
to. It wasn't insulting; in fact, it was quite flattering.
Still, his frank appraisal made her blush.

"We're meeting a realtor," he continued, "and we

may look at some houses that can best be reached by boat to get a true feeling for them."

"No kidding?" Valentine asked, genuinely surprised. "We really *are* going house hunting, aren't we?"

"Now, what did you think we were going to do?" he teased, mischief in his dark eyes. "Am I being naive? Did you have something more in mind, and I wasn't perceptive enough to pick up on it?"

This time Valentine's face turned scarlet. "No, Raleigh! I just meant that I thought we'd look at a couple of houses off the streets, just like in any other area."

"Oh," he murmured, pretending to be extremely disappointed. "All business again. Tsk. Tsk. That's too bad."

"I'm just along to give you a woman's opinion," she said, feeling terribly silly at the turn of the conversation. "Remember?"

His gaze roved over her again. "How could I forget?"

"Raleigh, now you stop that!" Valentine said, truly flustered.

He laughed. "Ah, but my friend, you look exceptionally beautiful today." He reached out and let his fingers trail through her long blond waves. "Is that the new crimped style I've been hearing about?"

She laughed, breaking some of the budding tension as she brushed his hand away. "Not by any stretch of the imagination. It's what happens when I wear a braid all day and don't have time to wash and curl my hair before an appointment."

"Oh, Lord," he said, pretending total chagrin, "we'd better go before the situation starts to hurt my feelings.

I've degenerated from friend to 'appointment' again. And we do have the appointment with the realtor. Actually, part of the fun of looking at a place at the lake is because of the lake, so I'm glad she's going to show us some of it by boat. Are you ready?"

She nodded, but honestly she didn't know if she would ever be ready for this man. He really was magnetic and mesmerizing. Well, at least there would be another person along to dampen her already rising ardor. And a woman at that. She should have known any realtor Raleigh picked would be female!

When they reached his car, Valentine pulled a five-dollar bill from her purse and handed it to him.

He looked at her curiously. "What's this?" he asked, eyes sparkling teasingly. "Please! You don't have to pay me for my company! And even if that's your intention, five dollars is rather an insult, isn't it?"

Valentine started laughing. "Raleigh, you're crazy! You're impossible. If I were paying for your company, I wouldn't give you two cents!"

"Now you're trying to hurt my feelings again," he said, mock pain in his eyes. "Two cents! I know I'm getting old, but good heavens, woman!"

"Will you stop it?" she said, still laughing. "This is the money you left on the table after breakfast yesterday. The coffee and brownies didn't cost that much and were my treat anyway. Besides, talk about hurt feelings. You didn't even eat your brownie! Am I to assume you didn't like it after I slaved over a hot oven all morning?"

It was Raleigh's turn to laugh as he opened the car and helped her in. "Talk about turning the tables," he murmured, reaching inside to buckle her seat belt across her waist, causing her pulse to race again as he bent over her.

"I'll be honest with you, lady. I was so interested in you and so determined that you not escape that I didn't even know there were brownies on the table. I certainly don't want the five dollars back. It was worth it just to see you. I'm sure the brownies were delicious, but you were more so."

Then, before Valentine could even begin to think coherently, his lips lightly brushed hers. She drew in a shuddering breath as he went around to the driver's side of the car.

He was so appealing! How was she going to get through this day—even with another woman along? Her heart was pounding and she was trembling inside. She tried her best to remember that he was a man skilled in careless flattery, but it was hard. Damned hard. She *wanted* to believe every single word!

The drive to Smith Mountain Lake was lovely; the winding tree-lined roads and hills provided beautiful scenery and a much-needed topic to distract them both from the almost palpable tension that had filled the car after Raleigh's brief kiss.

Valentine could swear that her lips were still tingling. She was sure of it each time she opened her mouth to speak, and it seemed so utterly ridiculous that she tried not to look at Raleigh at all. Each new crest of each new hill brought about another exclamation of how pretty the landscape was. She clung adamantly to the subject like a drowning woman, and Raeligh obliged her by agreeing with her assessment of the countryside.

"I think it's beautiful, too," he assured her. "I can

understand why Randolph is so taken with it. He and
Mimmi will keep working at the restaurant, but he says
he won't mind commuting at all."

"Does he know you're getting him a house for a
wedding present?" Valentine asked.

"No! It's a secret," Raleigh declared solemnly.
"Don't breathe a word of it. Even Carolyn and Tod
don't know. That's why I'm so grateful you're with me
to help me select something. I really don't know what a
young woman might find appealing in a house, what
features she might prefer over others."

"Well, it does depend on the woman, of course,"
Valentine said logically.

Raleigh nodded. "Yes, but I can tell you have an eye
for what's good. I love the way you've done your
shop."

Valentine was inordinately flattered by the compliment. Dammit! she told herself. Why did everything he
said please her so much?

"How do you know I decorated it?" she asked a little
flippantly.

He winked. "It looks like you. It's sunny and fresh,
and it has a special homey warmth to it. I'm sure your
customers feel comfortable and linger much longer than
they might elsewhere just because of the feeling of welcome the bakery has—not to mention the wonderful
way it smells! You did do it, didn't you?"

"Yes," she admitted, again inordinately pleased. She
did think comfort and a welcoming atmosphere were the
two most important qualities any place could have, be it
a home or shop.

"You have a decorator's touch, you know," he said.

"I hate those sterile cold places. I want to get out of them as fast as possible. But I love your shop. I liked it the moment I stepped inside."

"Thank you."

Valentine quickly changed the subject again to the beauty all around them. Raleigh's compliments inevitably embarrassed as well as flattered her. "You really must see this land when the leaves are changing colors. That's the only time I've been up here, and the sight was breathtaking."

"I'm sure it was," he agreed, taking his gaze off the road to look at her for a moment.

Although she was acutely aware of him watching her, Valentine pretendeed immense interest in the view outside the window. She could feel her silly heart begin to pound again. Why, oh why did this man have such a strong effect on her? The car felt too small to contain them.

She was relieved when Raleigh stopped by a small realty office. "Janie will take us around," he said, getting out of the car.

Valentine waited until he'd opened her door, knowing that the thrill of his fingers around hers would send those shivers up and down her spine again. When he continued to hold her hand while he took her into the office, she didn't protest although she knew she should.

A sharp-looking, dark-haired woman in her thirties glanced up when Raleigh walked in. He ushered Valentine forward with his warm fingers on her back.

"You have to be Raleigh Coseegan!" the woman exclaimed effusively and familiarly. "Right on time, as I should have known you would be. You didn't have any trouble finding me, did you?"

He shook his head. "I brought my trusty guide with me. She's going to give me her invaluable opinion. Janie Rossman, this is Valentine Smith."

Janie smiled enthusiastically, yet Valentine had the feeling once again, as she had had with Genna in the Italian restaurant, that Janie wished Raleigh was alone.

"Pleased to meet you, I'm sure," Janie said a little too perfunctorily. She extended her hand to Valentine and firmly shook hands. Then she turned to Raleigh and did the same, her fingers lingering slightly longer.

"I'm delighted we'll have a second opinion," Janie said, "but as we discussed on the phone several times, you're paying me to do my best for you, Raleigh, and I assure you that I won't let you down. At least, no one has been disappointed yet." Her dark eyes flashed. "I've been so eager to meet you. I've read some of your work."

"I'm sure no one's been disappointed with your services," Raleigh said, clearly undaunted by the fact that the woman was obviously giving him a double message. She had hoped he would come alone; she made it very clear.

Valentine let her gaze wander over the tall, dark beauty and wondered if Raleigh regretted not coming by himself now that he'd met the woman. As though he could read her mind, he reached for her hand.

"We're ready to see houses when you're ready to show them," he said smoothly, ignoring the woman's bold appraisal of him and her flattery about his work.

"Fine." Her smile was excessively bright. "I'll just

get my purse. I have a list of several places to show you."

When she'd closed the shop and led them to a big Cadillac, she suggested, "Why don't you sit in front with me, Raleigh, since you're the prospective buyer and will be able to see better?"

He smiled at her. "Thank you, but I'll be able to see just fine from the back seat. I believe Valentine will be more comfortable in front."

"Fine," Janie said brightly.

Valentine had the feeling it wasn't fine at all. She sighed. She didn't know how she would cope with all the interest other women showed in Raleigh were a romance to develop between them. She'd never really considered herself the jealous type, but she was acutely aware of what a ladies' man Raleigh was.

She brushed the thought aside. It was premature, ridiculous! And dangerous!

When they had been seated in the plush car, Janie looked over her shoulder at Raleigh and smiled. "There are, of course, all kinds of price ranges here at the lake. I've selected six homes that seem to meet your specifications. We have other options if none of these suit you."

"Fine," he said, leaning forward a bit and smiling at her. "I'm sure we'll find something. Valentine and I love the area already and agree that it would be a lovely place to live."

Janie glanced at Valentine a bit oddly. Valentine herself drew in her breath. *They* loved the area already! The way Raleigh had said it seemed strange when they were talking about a house for Randolph and Mimmi.

Valentine had thought she was the only one who noticed, but obviously Janie had also. They both were probably reading something into a harmless comment.

"Are you interested in a home here, too?" Janie asked. The dazzling smile that had been reserved for Raleigh only was now turned on Valentine.

She knew she was blushing and felt extremely foolish. "No, really, I'm just along for the ride with Raleigh."

In the back seat, Raleigh chuckled. "Don't let her fool you, Janie. She's the one who's going to select the house."

Valentine glanced back at him. "Really, Raleigh, I don't even know Randolph and Mimmi."

He smiled broadly at her. "You'll do just fine. Just fine, and we'll all be happy."

She turned back around and knew that the blush was deepening on her cheeks. She wondered if he was teasing her, but he seemed very, very serious.

Unfortunately, they all soon discovered that Valentine was very little help. Janie showed them three houses near the entrance to the lake, not even on the water, but nearby and with splendid views. Valentine fell in love with all of them. She just couldn't resist each one.

"You're not much help," Raleigh joked when she exclaimed over the third one as enthusiastically as she had over the first two.

"I'm sorry," she said earnestly. "They're just so beautiful."

He grinned at her. "Well, let's see what else Janie has to show us. Maybe we'll make the decision by selecting the one you exclaim over the most."

Valentine could only smile. She did love all the houses they had seen. "I warned you," she said as they went back out to the car. "You're going to have to decide, whether you want to or not. This is like being in a bakery shop for me. Everything looks delicious."

Raleigh laughed, but he found himself thinking that Valentine herself was the only thing he'd seen that was delicious. He couldn't stop comparing her to Janie, who was so cool and knowledgeable, while Valentine rushed around, eyes aglow, like a happy child in a toy shop.

The houses were nice, very nice without exception, and probably any one would do, but what interested him was Valentine's excitement. He loved the way she hesitated at the doorway of each new room as she peered into it in anticipation, or raced up the steps and gazed out the windows at the water. He believed that she would be happy here herself. That mattered to him.

Finally Janie drove them down to the dock, where a deckhand waited on her own boat to give them a tour of the lake and the other homes she wanted them to see. Valentine was all aglow, a smile on her face, the wind in her hair, thoroughly enjoying the excursion.

When they worked their way back into a cove where they docked and went up three flights of steps to a lovely little A-frame two-story cottage, Valentine cried, "Oh, this is it, Raleigh. This one is really it! They'll love this one."

He and Janie both laughed. They hadn't even gone inside. "Shall I sign a contract now, or do you think we should take a look in the house?" he drawled.

Valentine felt ridiculous, but when she saw his indulgent smile, she knew he wasn't making fun of her.

"Of course," she said, "I wouldn't buy anything without seeing it first. It's just that—"

Words failed her. She knew that she loved the house, even without seeing the inside. She couldn't explain it, and to try would sound stupid. But she thought it was silly for him to put such stock in her opinion anyway. She really didn't know the wedding couple!

"It's just that this *is* the house, isn't it?" Raleigh said perceptively. "This is the house you would choose, without even going inside."

"Some people do just sense these things," Janie interjected eagerly. "They feel an instant rapport with the house. I've sold couples houses when they've only seen pictures, and they've been ecstatic when they do actually go into the house."

Valentine was grateful for the other woman's support, regardless of whether she was telling the truth or only trying to make a sale.

"Well, let's see if she keeps her enthusiasm when we check out the house," Raleigh said, still smiling.

Valentine vowed to herself that she would not ooh and ahh over the place, no matter how wonderful she found it to be, but that wasn't the case when Janie opened the door. The cottage was exquisite. She was wild about it. And there was no way she could contain herself. She hurried from room to room, more eager to see the next than the last.

Raleigh shook his head and followed. Janie kept pace with Valentine, obviously knowing instinctively it was Valentine's opinion that would matter. Janie kept up a running commentary on the positive points, including beauty and accessibility from both the road and the water.

"We'll take it," Raleigh said when the tour was over. "Obviously the lady knows this is the house."

"Raleigh!" Valentine cried, realizing that he was absolutely serious about letting her pick out the house, "I don't know if Randolph and Mimmi will like it. Please don't buy it on my say-so."

"Yours is as good as mine," he said. "If they don't like it, they can always sell later."

"So true," Janie agreed, eager to encourage the buy.

"Shouldn't we see the others Janie mentioned?" Valentine asked, frowning.

"Yes, I fully intend to see them. I may be interested," Raleigh said. "But I'm buying this one."

Valentine and Janie exchanged glances. Although Valentine didn't know what the other woman was thinking, she herself suddenly had a thousand butterflies in her stomach.

Why was Raleigh going to look at the other houses if he was buying this one? What did it mean—he may be interested? Was one for him? Could he possibly be serious about settling down in the area? And why had he let her decide on the house?

She shook her head. She was overreacting again. However, the butterflies only increased as they left the cottage and headed back to the boat.

CHAPTER EIGHT

JANIE TOOK THEM to several other houses on the water. Despite being enthusiastic about each of them, Valentine felt that none compared to the one Raleigh had said he was going to buy. Still, he kept questioning her, asking her which of the houses she would choose if she hadn't decided on the first one at the cove.

Puzzled by his persistence, she finally decided that maybe he would let cost be the determining factor; with two houses to bargain for instead of one, he would have an advantage. She really did like another cottage on the water, with easy access from the highway, but not as well as the one at the cove. The house was enchanting and she truly believed that a young couple would be thrilled with it. Heaven knows she would have been.

In fact, she was extraordinarily impressed with Raleigh's generosity where Randolph and Mimmi were concerned. She was aware that they had money problems and that housing was the biggest cost anyone faced.

She couldn't help but be reminded that if she didn't have house payments, she wouldn't be in such a bind now that Mr. Carruthers had raised the rent. The old goat! she thought resentfully.

"We have other places to see if you're interested," Janie said, her voice high and animated, startling Valentine from her thoughts.

Raleigh shook his head. "The lady has worked all day," he said. "I think we've found the houses we like best."

"Houses?" Janie murmured, flashing her dazzling smile again.

Valentine could almost see dollar signs in the woman's eyes. Apparently she had given up all personal interest in Raleigh, but she sure thought she was on to something with the "houses." Valentine didn't understand it herself; she was as curious as Janie to see if Raleigh really meant the plural. Her foolish heart began that frustratingly mad beating.

Raleigh chuckled. "Well, I really didn't know what a young couple might like. Valentine is more in tune with that sort of thing than I am, but I have left myself the option of final say on the house."

Janie and Valentine both stared at him. "Pardon me," Janie said smoothly, "did I misunderstand? Aren't you going to buy the cottage at the cove? Have you changed your mind about that one?"

"Not at all," Raleigh said just as smoothly. "I'm taking that one. I agree with Valentine that it's the most appealing, but I also liked her second choice. I was interested to see what else she would select." He winked at Valentine. "See how much we have in common?"

She nodded, feeling ridiculously let down. So Raleigh had been in control all the time. She hadn't really been the sole selector of the wedding couple's house. It just happened that she and Raleigh had been in accord on what they liked in homes. She told herself that she should have had enough sense to realize that Raleigh wasn't going to let a stranger pick out a house for his relatives. And that's what she was: a stranger.

Janie seemed equally let down. She forced a bright artificial laugh. "To be perfectly frank, Mr. Coseegan," she said, suddenly reverting to a more formal tone with him, "I thought you were considering buying *both* cottages."

"I did consider them both," he said. "However, I really think the one at the cove is the right one."

"Good," Janie said, apparently trying to be gracious and satisfied with the single sale, in spite of her disappointment. "We'll just stop by the house and sign the contract."

"I'll come back tomorrow," Raleigh said. "Valentine needs to get home." He glanced at his watch. It was getting late and he knew Valentine needed her sleep so she could get up early for work. He wanted to spend a little more time with her himself, and they had the ride back to town.

"It will only take a moment," Janie said hurriedly, wanting to make the sale now while it sounded like a sure thing.

"Tomorrow," Raleigh said firmly, leaving no room for contradiction.

Janie smiled. "That will be fine, of course."

Valentine felt foolishly deflated. Although it was silly of her, she realized she'd wanted to be in on the whole thing. She'd wanted to see Raleigh actually purchase the house for the bride and groom. She thought the entire event was incredibly sweet and romantic, and she was pleased that she'd been a part of it, even if she hadn't played as large a part as she had initially imagined.

When they were back in Raleigh's car, he asked, "What would be the best time for you to meet with the family, the florist, and Maria? We really need to get underway with these plans since the affair has gotten so large."

"I agree wholeheartedly," Valentine said, feeling a slight surge of fresh panic. "The sooner the better, although Lucy and I have already been working on ideas."

"Great! How about tomorrow night at seven? Maria's restaurant is closed and we can all meet at Tod and Carolyn's restaurant."

"That will be fine," Valentine agreed.

Raleigh glanced over at her. "Now, you don't feel that I'm imposing too much, do you? Rushing you?"

"Oh, for heaven's sake no! This is business; we need to get organized. There's so little time left for such a huge endeavor."

Raleigh thought the same thing; he had not only the wedding to contend with, he was also trying to convince this woman that she was as interested in him as he was in her. He honestly didn't know how much convincing that would take.

"Will you have time to make my birthday cake by Friday?" he asked, glancing away, hoping Valentine couldn't tell he was getting ready to fib to her when he had so recently promised not to. "I would like to bring Carolyn and Tod out to the cottage to show it to them. We could have the cake there—the four of us—and celebrate my birthday early."

"Sure," Valentine said casually, foolishly thrilled by the idea, "but aren't the lights off at the cottage?"

He nodded. "Yes. We'll make it early in the evening." He looked down at his watch. "In fact," he said, snapping his fingers, "why don't I pick up some chicken and wine? We'll toast the bride and groom's new house. I think Carolyn and Tod would get a kick out of it."

Valentine laughed. She loved the idea. "No problem," she said gaily. "The cake and I will be ready at five when I close on Friday."

"Good," he said, smiling a little to himself. "Very good. Thank you for agreeing."

"I'm happy to do it, even if it is because I lost the bet. It sounds like fun," Valentine said honestly.

"It will be," Raleigh agreed. "I promise you that."

Looking at him, she wondered if there was a hidden message beneath his words; but then she was always off on the wrong track with this man, reading all kinds of things into his statements. She was just being silly again. She knew she *wanted* to believe there was more to what he was saying.

True to his word, Raleigh kept up the friendly status of their relationship when he walked Valentine to the door. He made no jokes about how tempting she was. He didn't even try to take her hand as they walked to the front porch.

"Thanks a lot for going with me to pick out houses," he said. "It means more to me than you can know."

"It was nothing," she said offhandedly. "I enjoyed it. They were all lovely, weren't they?"

"That they were," he said. "You're sure the one at the cove is the one you would choose."

"Yes, but as I said, Raleigh, I'd choose it for myself. I don't know what Randolph and Mimmi will like."

She knew now that she was glad he hadn't left the entire responsibility for selecting the house on her shoulders. She would feel terrible if the young couple was disappointed, although she couldn't imagine anyone not being ecstatic with any house an uncle *gave* them.

"I'm glad you said you agreed with me on that particular one," she added.

"It's a wonderful house," he said. "I'm very pleased that we like the same kind of home. That made it all so much easier."

She smiled. "What we like isn't what counts, is it? Still, I simply can't imagine anyone not being thrilled with the cottage, especially someone receiving it as a wedding gift. Raleigh, I think you're so generous to do this."

He laughed. "Now be careful. I'll start thinking you're impressed with me again, and who knows where that might lead."

Valentine *was* impressed with him. Heaven knew she was, but she was just too afraid of where he might lead her. She already knew her heart was in jeopardy.

When she didn't comment, Raleigh said, "See you at the restaurant at seven tomorrow night, if you're sure that's all right."

"It's fine," she said with a smile. "Really it is. I'm very excited about the wedding arrangements. I'm sure Lucy will want to come with me."

"Good." Suddenly Raleigh bent forward and lightly brushed Valentine's lips with his. "Good night."

Then he turned on his heel and was gone.

Valentine opened the door to her house and went inside. She was left with an empty feeling she couldn't explain even to herself. She had set up the friendship status; she had asked Raleigh not to rush her.

Yet she was more disappointed than she could recall being in a long, long time, and she had known some disappointments. What she had really wanted, she knew, was for Raleigh to pull her into his arms and kiss her as he had the first time.

What a fool she was! What a silly, silly fool! She was *asking* for heartache! She didn't know which hurt the most: not being at risk with Raleigh, or being at risk. As it was, she felt absolutely miserable. She went to bed with tears trailing down her cheeks.

She didn't know what she wanted. Her life had just begun to settle down when he barged into it. And what now? Oh, Lord, what now?

The meeting at the restaurant the next night went very well, despite the fact that it was held in the same room where Valentine did her infamous belly dance. Her breath caught in her throat when she was ushered inside, but soon she managed to settle down and get caught up in the excitement of the wedding plans.

The room was bustling with animated faces and lively voices. Carolyn and Tod had invited all the others who were participating, including the people who were going to supply additional food and beverages for the expected numerous guests.

Valentine was relieved to see Raleigh when he sat down beside her. Although she recognized this as another golden opportunity to make connections for her bakery, she was a little nervous. Lucy had decided that Valentine must do this alone; even though Valentine fervently disapproved, the other woman wouldn't budge.

Lucy would have fit in fine, Val told herself when she saw those assembled. Some of the elderly ladies who were so excitedly talking about the cookies they were bringing were the shapers of local society. Valentine knew that was part of the reason Lucy had insisted she come alone, so that she would be forced to stop being an outsider, hiding behind Lucy in her dealings with the locals.

With his usual confidence, Raleigh pulled his chair close to Valentine's, put his arm on the back of hers, and began the discussion of the momentous occasion. After listening awhile, Valentine enthusiastically talked about her intended contributions, all of which were met with much enthusiasm.

By the time the meeting ended, everyone was feeling good about the upcoming nuptials. There would, of course, be the inevitable minor errors in judgment, but the event seemed remarkably well planned with all the key people aware of what they were supposed to do.

The minister had said that some of the people from the congregation wanted to bring food, too, so it was agreed that individuals who wished to do so could bring food instead of gifts for the bride and groom. Only the immediate family and the closest of friends were encouraged to give gifts; otherwise it was beginning to sound as if the young couple would receive enough presents to open a department store.

Everyone was in an extraordinarily good mood as they departed. The bride and groom were radiant, and for the first time in many days, Carolyn seemed confident and relaxed about the wedding. She was glad she had decided to include more of the town, for they really seemed to enjoy the idea.

"Can I see you home?" Raleigh asked Valentine when they had reached her car in the restaurant parking lot.

She longed to say yes, but it was late and she was feeling more vulnerable than usual with him. He had been beside her every step of the way tonight, encouraging her to come forth with all her ideas, no matter how far out they seemed.

Buoyed by his confidence, she had pressed ahead with innovative ideas, matched with the florists' planned decor. Still, the fact was that she had leaned on Raleigh far more than she had meant to; without him at her side, she never would have been so bold.

"I don't think so," she forced herself to say. "I'm tired."

She could see that he was disappointed, but he smiled. "Friday, then. Five o'clock with my cake. Don't forget."

"I won't," she assured him. She had already planned an amusing cake for him; she was looking forward to the birthday celebration with great enthusiasm. "Make it about fifteen minutes after five," she said.

"Fine." He lightly brushed her forehead with his lips, then turned toward his own car. Valentine gazed after him for a moment, wishing already that she had said yes, instead of no, to his seeing her home.

But Friday was only five days away. She would see him then. Her pulse raced at the thought. Thank God, Carolyn and Tod were going to be there. Only heaven knew what would happen if Raleigh and Valentine were in the cottage all alone. Her resolve to proceed cautiously dissolved the moment he touched her.

Friday did come rapidly. The days between passed in a blur. Two of the society women from the meeting at Tod and Carolyn's restaurant asked Valentine to cater their social spring flings. She knew instinctively that she was on her way with her bakery. Soon it wouldn't matter how much old Mr. Carruthers raised the rent.

Anyway, she *would* move as soon as the business began to show a profit. It was a matter of principle with her, no matter how much she loved the building and the location. Mr. Carruthers wasn't going to get away with trying to blackmail her! She wasn't ever going to be in that position again.

As before, Valentine had brought along a change of clothes; she freshened herself in the shop restroom after she'd locked up at five. Before she left for work that morning, she had taken care with her hair in anticipation of the occasion tonight. She took off her hairnet and let casual blond curls flow down her back. Liking the effect, she brushed her hair lightly.

Then she slipped on the full-skirted blue dress and matching hose she'd purchased especially for this evening. The last time she'd worn a dress for Raleigh, she'd felt dowdy. She wanted tonight to be different. After all, it was special. The cake was ready, and so was she, she decided, glancing in the mirror.

When Raleigh knocked on the door at five-fifteen, she hurried to let him in. She was surprised to see that he was alone.

"Hi," she said, her heart taking up the erratic beat that signaled Raleigh's appearance and its effect upon her.

"Hi," he returned. "Lord, you look lovely tonight!"

Valentine felt that now-familiar betraying blush. "Thank you. Where are Carolyn and Tod?" Her sentences ran together.

Raleigh gave her a rueful expression. "I hope you aren't going to be too disappointed. I'm afraid it's just you and me tonight to celebrate my brithday."

He met her eyes, knowing that he was going to lie to her, but not completely. His sister *was* terrible at keeping surprises.

"I hinted at my surprise and I realized that Carolyn would never be able to keep it to herself. I'm afraid she'll ruin everything if I show her and Tod the place beforehand."

"Oh," Valentine said, her emotions suddenly swirling in confusion. On the one hand, she was well aware that she was happy to think only she and Raleigh would share his birthday; on the other, she wondered what their evening alone together would bring.

"Tell me you still want to help me celebrate," Raleigh coaxed.

"I do," she quickly assured him, because it was certainly the truth. She laughed nervously. "We have a lot of cake, and I do mean a lot."

He laughed too. "We don't have to eat it all tonight, you know. We have a lot of chicken and wine, also."

They both laughed as she led him to the kitchen where the birthday cake was. It was boxed, and when Raleigh tried to open it, Valentine rapped his knuckles with hers.

"No, you can't look at it until we're ready to eat it!" she insisted.

He chuckled as he caught her fingers in his. "That's fine with me. Are you ready to go?"

She nodded, then hesitated. "Where are we going, now that you aren't taking Carolyn and Tod to the cottage?"

Gazing down at his fingers intertwined with hers, she vacillated over whether she should invite him to her place. Actually, she'd had her heart set on seeing the cottage again.

He seemed pensive for a moment, then said, "Why don't we go on as we'd planned, if that's all right with you. I signed the contract, but I do want to go back to the cottage and see it again."

He glanced around the shop and laughed as he lightly squeezed her fingers. "In fact, to tell you the truth, I'm hoping you'll help me with it a little more. I don't care at all for the blinds, and I'd like new carpet in the living

room. I'm hopeless with colors, and obviously you do
so well."

Valentine slipped her fingers from his and picked up
the boxed cake. She was flattered—again—and she
didn't want him to know how his touch caused her to
tingle and tremble.

Her gaze involuntarily swept over him. Nor did she
want to say that he didn't seem to have any trouble at all
with colors. Tonight he was dressed in beige slacks that
emphasized his lean hips and blatantly masculine phy-
sique and a cocoa-colored shirt that molded to the defined lines of his chest and set off his dark eyes and
blond hair. He wore brown loafers that matched his thin
brown belt perfectly.

Thinking that she was reluctant, Raleigh said
quickly, "I know I've asked a lot of you, what with all
you have to do to get ready for the wedding. I'll give
you a key so you can go to the cottage when it's conve-
nient for you. It really would be a big help to me. I just
don't feel competent to do it, and I'm afraid I'll give
away what I hope will be a fine surprise if I discuss it
with Carolyn or try to find out Mimmi's preferred
colors."

"I'd be happy to help." She smiled at him. "I do like
to think I have an eye for color and, after all, what are
friends for?"

"What indeed?" he murmured.

The way he said it inexplicably sent a shiver racing
up Valentine's spine.

When they reached the cottage, Valentine felt goose
bumps on her skin. It was the oddest feeling in the

world, but she felt as if *she* belonged in this cottage. For a brief moment, she pretended that Raleigh had bought it for her. But only for a moment. She knew she was being silly again.

"You really do love this place, don't you?" Raleigh asked.

Valentine smiled. "Raleigh Coseegan, why do I think you can read my mind? Do you have psychic powers?"

He laughed. "How I wish I did. It would make my life, my world, so much easier." I would know where I stood with you, he silently told himself, and what I want to do with my future—our future.

He laughed again. "I've told you, Valentine, that I'll try my best to be truthful with you. Woman, much of what you think and feel shows up in those pretty blue eyes of yours as though they were a mirror to your soul. You love this house. It's written there for anyone to see. I can't tell you how that pleases me."

Valentine smiled nervously and wondered what else was visible in her eyes. "I'm sorry I'm so transparent. I'm told that takes the mystery out of a woman for a man, and all men love the mystery."

"Not all men," he said flatly. "I'm so weary of games that I can't even begin to tell you. I'm beginning to long for the simple life, a life where people can just be people, where they aren't trying to outsmart each other or hurt each other for political profit or worse—for money."

He looked into her eyes. "I'm sorry. Please forgive my philosophical digression. This is supposed to be a fun occasion. After all, it's a birthday party."

Valentine tried to smile. She wasn't sorry at all that

Raleigh had opened up to her. It gave her more hope that he might indeed be ready to settle down in a simple small southern town, that he might be ready to give up his wandering life.

She caught herself just in time. She was daydreaming again. And only because she wanted Raleigh to settle down—*for her!* Even if the man did stay in this area, he would do so because of his obvious love for his family. There were thousands of little towns he could choose otherwise.

"How can this be a birthday party with only two of us?" she asked playfully, wanting to lighten the mood.

"Are you serious?" he asked. "A party for two is the very best kind. That I promise you!"

When Valentine met his eyes, she had no doubt that a party for two with this man would indeed be a memorable event, but she only smiled again. "And who's going to eat all this cake?"

"Can we freeze it?" he asked, seeming quite serious. "How about sharing some of it with the guests at the wedding? It does look like a huge cake!"

Valentine laughed. "That's what you wanted, mister, and that is what I delivered. You haven't even seen it! It's four layers!"

"Is that all?" he teased. "Well, in that case, maybe I'll be able to eat it all myself tonight. No problem!"

They both laughed. Valentine began to relax, but only a little. She liked Raleigh so much that her joy was always mingled with pain. She was ever on guard that he was going to go away and hurt her just when she needed and wanted him most. That he was going away was inevitable, but did she have to fall in love with him before he left?

Shivers raced across her skin again. Surely she wasn't that much of a fool. Surely! But something told her she was. Something else told her she was already in love.

Her stomach clenched uncomfortably, and she wondered if she could even participate in the party. Her emotions were churning and the combination of ecstasy and anxiety was almost her undoing.

Raleigh opened the car door and climbed out. "Now I insist on carrying everything into the house—even the cake," he said.

Valentine forced a laugh. She was suddenly shaking inside. "No way, mister. I'm carrying the cake. I don't want you peeking until *I* open it. I lost the bet and I'll reveal my payoff when the time is right."

He chuckled. "What am I going to do with you, Valentine Smith? What if you drop my four-layer cake and I never get to eat it?"

"No chance," she said. "I'm used to carrying cakes. You just get your other goodies, and I'll take care of my end of the food supply."

She had been holding the cake on her lap and she allowed Raleigh to take it while she got out of the car; then she waited while he got the boxes and bags from the back. She assumed that was the chicken and wine; he'd certainly brought enough for an army!

Once they were inside the cottage, Raleigh returned to the car and retrieved a beautiful blanket he'd purchased in his travels. It was plush and soft and Valentine

watched eagerly as he spread it out on the carpet in front
of the fireplace.

"I wish it were cool enough to have a fire—and that
we had something to build one with," he noted. "But
I'm afraid the night is a little too warm for that."

Even though Valentine smiled, she was secretly relieved. Raleigh was setting up an incredibly intimate
atmosphere for this birthday party, and she was responding much too well to it already. She stood back
and let him create a little world for them in the front
room of the wedding cottage.

Soon there were two rose-colored candles in elegant
candleholders on the mantel over the fireplace. The
blanket had been set like an elaborate table with honest-
to-goodness china and delicate wineglasses. Chicken
and potato salad were served on the lovely plates. Raleigh poured wine, then invited Valentine to sit down.

"I'll take this now," he said, reaching out for the cake
she hadn't even realized she was still holding. A four-
layer cake wasn't exactly light, but she'd been so engrossed in what Raleigh was doing that she'd forgotten
about the birthday cake.

"No peeking," she said, her voice suddenly and em-
barrassingly hoarse.

"Not even now?" he asked, managing to look woefully disappointed.

"Oh, all right," she said, relenting as he placed the
boxed cake alongside the other food.

When he opened the lid, he laughed delightedly.
"Well, you wicked little witch!" he cried. The cake was
shaped like an old man, complete with a cane, baggy
pants, fringes of white hair, and very obvious false

teeth. *Over the hill at thirty-seven and sliding!* was written across the bottom of the cake.

Valentine hadn't known how he would take the gag cake, but she was tickled with his response. "Well," she said with pretended nonchalance, "you boasted so much about looking good at thirty-six that I thought your ego needed a little deflating."

He chuckled again, then reached over to pull her into his arms. "Over the hill indeed! I'll show you how over the hill I am, woman."

Suddenly he pressed her back against the blanket and his mouth found hers to claim it with all the pent-up ardor he'd been feeling for days.

"Raleigh, you mustn't," Valentine whispered against his lips.

"Mustn't what?" he murmured as his tongue traced the shape of her mouth.

Valentine didn't have an answer to his question. She didn't even realize that she was the one who'd inspired it. Locking her arms around his neck, she drew him tighter to her and savored the feel of his hard body against her. She didn't know or care what was going on in the rest of the world.

CHAPTER NINE

VALENTINE REVELED IN the burning contact wherever Raleigh touched her. All she could think of was wanting more and more of him. She had hungered for him too long; in a single moment, all the reasons she had warned herself against this man were forgotten.

He was bold and sexy and exciting, and Lord help her, she was in love with him! She didn't know how long she'd known it, only that she *did* know it. Here and now, all she wanted was Raleigh, and the rest of the world and its opinion be damned.

He smothered her face with kisses and trailed his tongue along her neck. Valentine clung to him, wanting all that he had to offer, wanting all that he had to give. When his mouth found hers again, she savored the passionate joining of their lips.

His hands strayed down to her breasts and cupped

them sensuously even as his mouth continued to explore hers, his tongue tasting all the sweetness of the tender inside of her mouth.

When he began to unbutton her dress, Valentine shivered in delicious anticipation of what was to come. She had no doubt at all that Raleigh was about to take her where she'd never been, and she wanted to relish every step of the way.

Raleigh paused to look at her when she trembled, but Valentine didn't open her eyes. He wanted to read the expression there, but her body had already told him all he needed to know. She wanted him as much as he wanted her, if that was possible.

He opened her dress to expose her high, small breasts, clad only in a sheer lace bra. His tongue sought the nipple visible through the lace and he traced the hard bud, then sucked gently on it, sending rivers of sensation through Valentine.

Aching with desire, Valentine arched her back, wanting Raleigh to give her still more of the sensual pleasure of the touch of his tongue and lips, the feel of his body on hers. When he cupped and stroked her other breast, she moaned as maddeningly delicious thrills chased each other across her skin. She felt hot way down deep inside, as if she would never be cool again.

"I think we have too many barriers between us," Raleigh said thickly. "Let's get rid of some of these clothes, why don't we?"

Valentine couldn't even find her voice to answer. She didn't care what he did as long as he didn't stop creating that strange icy heat inside her. She throbbed with a longing she'd never known. Even if she had only this one time with Raleigh, she wanted to experience it to the ultimate. If it never came again, she would know what it was like to be loved by a man, in the most intimate and fulfilling sense of the word.

He slid the blue dress off her shoulders, then Valentine raised his hips so that he could move it down her legs. She was lying there before him in nylons, heels, blue bikini panties, and a blue lace bra.

"Lord, you're beautiful," he whispered reverently, "just as I knew you would be."

He unclasped her bra and began to lick her breasts, first one, then the other, sending new spasms deep inside Valentine. She tensed and trembled as he began to slide her nylons down her hips.

"Relax, my sweet," he murmured soothingly.

Valentine wanted very much to relax, but she was burning and shaking. Raleigh removed her nylons, lifting each of her feet as he did so, removing her shoe and placing a teasing kiss beneath her instep. Valentine unconsciously smiled. She'd never had anyone do such a thing, and it aroused and amused her.

"Like that?" Raleigh asked.

"I like everything you do," Valentine answered with naked truth, then blushed deeply.

Raleigh smiled. "Good, because I've only begun, but let me get out of these clothes. I want to feel my skin against yours."

Valentine wanted to help him as he had her, but she couldn't muster the nerve. She lay wide-eyed, watching while he exposed the most gorgeous male body she'd ever imagined. His desire for her was very visible, and still he took his time as he kneeled before her on the blanket.

He began to work his way up her legs, kissing and stroking, spreading her slim thighs to lightly kiss the tender insides.

Valentine thought for sure she would die from the tantalizing, provocative explorations he made of her body. She gasped when Raleigh eased his finger inside her to test her readiness for love, and when he arched himself over her and slowly joined his body with hers, she immediately cried out in joy.

Never in her wildest fantasies had she even imagined that she could experience such ecstasy. Every nerve ending in her body seemed to respond to his being inside her. She clasped his hips and urged him to plunge deeper, wanting him to quench the white-hot flames that burned somewhere deep, deep inside her. She knew he had the power to cool them, and she wanted that with every fiber of her being.

Raleigh had intended to take his time with her, to make love to her slowly and fully this first time, but her passion was such that he was driven to answer it. He thrust deeper and deeper as her hips hungrily met his to accept him.

In a matter of moments, they became lost in the joy and satisfaction only a man and woman can share so intimately. Raleigh had never known anything like it in his life. He was stunned and physically drained by the sensual experience, by Valentine's ability to give her love to him so fully.

He was a man of the world; he had slept with women who knew all there was to know about sex and the ways to please a man, but this sweet, vulnerable southern belle had taken him to a place he'd never been. He was truly moved by the experience. It was like something out of time and space, as if they had left the world behind. He didn't know any other way to describe it. He didn't think he could even try. He just lay there, his body still part of hers, and marveled in the wonder of it all.

"God, you're amazing," he finally whispered thickly as he caressed Valentine's damp hair and kissed her face and forehead. "I swear I've never known love like that before."

With all her heart Valentine wanted to believe him, but she was afraid. She wasn't fool enough not to know how naive she was about love. She could, however, in all honesty, tell him the same things he'd told her.

"And I swear I've never known love like that," she said a little shyly. "I didn't even know it could be like that."

She suspected in part that it was because she was in love with him and had wanted to give all of herself, whatever that was, to him; but the total experience had been more than anything she had thought possible.

Somewhere along the way it had gone beyond the physical and become almost spiritual. She wanted to say that to Raleigh, but she felt too silly to express herself in such a way.

To her horror, instead, three little words escaped from her lips. "I love you!" she barely breathed. Thank God, she said the words so softly that she wasn't even sure Raleigh heard them.

Raleigh rested his body on hers, wondering what she

had murmured. He wanted to ask her to repeat it, but he was afraid to spoil the moment, afraid that what he thought he'd heard wasn't anything near what she'd said.

Valentine could feel the savage beating of his heart, and she listened to her own echo it. Other than their pounding hearts, the room seemed to be filled with a heavy silence. She held her breath for a moment, wondering how Raleigh would respond to her confession of love, if he *would* respond.

Time seemed to stop while she waited. Raleigh said nothing at all. Valentine began to think the very worst. He *had* heard her confession of love and thought her a silly, stupid woman for telling him she loved him just because they'd made love.

Rising up to look down at her open, honest blue eyes, Raleigh murmured, "Valentine, I'm asking you to believe me when I tell you that it was more pleasurable than any experience I've ever had. I know you consider me a man of the world." He laughed nervously. "Hell, so do I, but I've never been moved by lovemaking like that. It was—it was—Hell, I'm a writer and I'm at a loss for words."

But he wasn't at a loss for words at all. It occurred to him that the experience had been so incomparable, so exquisite because he had gone and fallen in love with this woman! She was like no other he had ever met, and he relished that about her.

Still, he was truly afraid to say that he loved her—yet. Really afraid! He would laugh, but it wasn't funny. With love came commitment, and he still wasn't sure he was quite ready.

Oh, of course he had planned ahead already; he had given considerable thought to settling down in this town, writing books and eventually marrying—Valentine—he realized. That's why he'd bought two cottages, the one Valentine loved most for himself and perhaps her, and the other for his nephew and bride.

But, of course, in the back of his mind he knew the cottage was a good investment; if his plans didn't work out, he could always use the place as a retreat, or sell it.

Hell! All of this had gotten away from him. He was doing it all in reverse. He was supposed to get his assignment over with, settle down first, find the woman he wanted to spend the rest of his life with, fall in love with her, and make her part of his future. He still had that final assignment that he couldn't even tell Valentine about—and he knew in his heart that how he felt about that assignment would determine his future.

Or at least he had thought all that before he made love to this precious woman beneath him. His mind was a muddle. He had promised he wouldn't rush her. Everything was getting out of hand. Suddenly he moved away from her.

Valentine felt as if an icy wind had blown into the room; she reached for her dress to cover her nakedness. Raleigh had changed in that single moment: she'd said too much. He'd heard her love confession after all, and now she was sure he regretted making love to her. That's why he'd spent so much time trying to tell her how pleasurable the experience was. Pleasurable—and nothing more.

She would never regret that she'd made love with him, she knew. At least she would never regret the act;

she was sure she would live to regret the pain that would inevitably come.

His back to her, Raleigh said quietly, "Valentine, I had wanted this all to be different. I wanted to make love to you—I think I've wanted to since the first time I met you, but I had intended to take things much slower." He looked over his shoulder and met her eyes.

To Valentine's utter humiliation, she began to cry like the inexperienced little fool she was. She tried desperately to contain her tears, but suddenly she couldn't seem to stop sobbing. Raleigh *was* sorry he'd made love to her and it was more than she could bear at the moment.

"Oh, God," he said thickly, "please, don't cry. I didn't say that at all like I meant it," he said soothingly, placatingly. "Good God, woman, it's just happened so fast. I'm in love with you, and it's way too soon."

To her utter horror, he was adding insult to injury by lying to her just because he thought she would feel better if he said he loved her too. Of course she wasn't stupid enough to believe he was telling her for any other reason than because he felt obligated to after she'd said it to him. The ecstasy she'd felt minutes ago ebbed into agony. Sobbing and shaking, Valentine only wanted to run away.

As quickly as she could, she pulled on her dress and grabbed up her lingerie. "Please take me home," she said without even looking at him.

Raleigh tried to draw her back against his body, but Valentine was already escaping. "Please stay and listen," he pleaded plantively. "I'll try to explain all this the best I can, Valentine. Don't run away again. Don't run right now when the time is so critical."

She looked back at him with the most painful look he'd ever seen in anybody's eyes, he who had seen the wounded and dying. "Please take me home, Raleigh. Please."

He was stirred to his soul by her plea. He didn't have any idea how to salvage the evening—he, man of the world, man of the moment, able to work his way through almost any crisis.

Moments ago, this had been the most wonderful event in his life. Now it was a debacle. It had fallen apart around him as surely as though a bomb had been dropped on them both.

There was no point in talking. He was experienced enough in critical situations to know this woman wouldn't listen to anything he had to say. What she needed more than anything in the world right now was to go home, as she had asked, because that was what she thought she wanted in her heart.

With leaden fingers, Raleigh dressed. Valentine was waiting out on the porch for him when he had blown out the candles on the mantel, given one final forlorn look at the untouched birthday party food, and closed the door behind him. It was growing dark outside. That was a relief for them both.

The tension in the car was palpable as they made the return trip to town. It seemed to Raleigh that the drive back was twice as long as the drive up. He knew Valentine was anguished, and he knew he was the cause. It hurt right to his soul to believe that she thought all the wrong things—or even worse, not to be sure just what she thought.

He knew he shouldn't, but he had to try to explain again. He just didn't know what to explain. Should he tell her that he'd bought the cottage they'd just left because it was the one she wanted, and because he thought she was the woman he wanted? Because he wanted to live there with her?

And what happened if he did go on the assignment and find that he couldn't give up his way of life after all? What if this woman and this time away from his other life had refreshed him so that he could face it all again—worse yet, that he wanted to face it?

What then? Oh, he had no doubt at all that he loved Valentine Smith and that she was the woman he wanted to marry. But his life was such that if he remained in his profession, he couldn't offer her marriage.

He ran his hands through his hair. God knew he didn't understand how everything had gone so wrong. He had intended to take things slowly. After all, he had only this single assignment left, critical though it was, and then he had truly hoped to make a final decision, a decision that would affect the rest of his life—and Valentine's, should she say yes to his proposal.

He had no choice but to try again. He couldn't let her go home in utter misery and dejection, knowing that he had inadvertently caused her unhappiness, especially after that bastard, Brady, and what he'd done to her. Raleigh couldn't help but recall his promise to her that she wouldn't regret her association with him.

"Valentine, we have to talk right now before this gets worse than it is. It's not what it seems. I do love you. That's no lie," he said fervently.

Her hands clenched almost prayerfully, Valentine

pressed them against her churning stomach and tried to hold herself together. It was better that she learned now of Raleigh's full power to hurt her than have it happen after she'd spent even more time with him.

"We slept together, Raleigh," she said in the cool, crisp voice that he despised right to the depths of his being. "I meant no more to you than any other one-night stand. Please don't make this any harder with your lies and attempts at deception."

"Valentine—"

She met his eyes. "I knew right from the start that I was out of your league. I don't regret what we did, but I don't need any more excuses or explanations."

God in heaven knew that she didn't regret giving herself to him. The price would be high, but the pleasure had been incomparable.

"Valentine, for heaven's sake, you must know you weren't just another one-night stand. I do love you. I have this one more—"

"Please," she said earnestly, "don't say any more. You don't need to treat me like the simple little southern belle you think I am. False words and foolish promises won't make it any different. We have to work together through the wedding; then I don't ever want to see or hear from you again." She laughed bitterly. "Not that I expect to, you understand."

He reached for her hand, but she moved it away. "Dammit, Valentine, listen to me."

"No!" she said tightly. "No more. I don't want to hear any more!"

Fast losing his own temper and knowing that

wouldn't help, Raleigh tightened his jaw muscles and gripped the wheel, driving much too fast on the curving road. This damned woman was making him crazy. Simple southern belle indeed! She was anything but simple; she was everything—everything he'd ever wanted. She was—oh, God, he didn't even know anymore what she was or what he wanted to say.

Suddenly a blue flashing light came on behind him. "Damn!" he cursed savagely, venting some of his frustration as he glanced down at the speedometer. He was doing sixty-five in a fifty-five zone. He hadn't even noticed how fast he was driving. His foot had been heavy, like his mind.

He pulled over to the side of the road, wishing he had somebody to take out his anger on. He hadn't had a ticket since he was sixteen, and he'd been in plenty of situations that warranted one.

Suddenly he smiled. He supposed he was long overdue, and actually he needed the distraction at the moment. He glanced over at Valentine and her eyes were wide with dismay.

"It's okay," he said. "I deserve it."

The young state trooper who came up to the car didn't look a day over twenty-two. "Your license and registration, sir," he said in a very authoritative voice.

Raleigh smiled again. He'd been stopped at borders of warring countries. This was easy.

The young man appeared overwhelmed by Raleigh's identification. Suddenly he was rather flustered. "Did you know that you were doing sixty-five in a fifty-five zone, sir?" the young man asked.

Raleigh shook his head. "To tell you the truth, officer, I was all in a turmoil over the love of this lady, and I didn't realize I was going so fast."

"Well, sir, I really should give you a summons," the trooper said. He looked into the car and his eyes met Valentine's teary blue ones. "But this time I'm going to let you off with a warning," he said, sounding much less authoritative. "If you want to live to see another birthday, keep your speed down on the highway and pay attention to your driving. More accidents are caused by people not paying attention than you'd imagine."

Raleigh almost smiled at that. He had probably seen more accidents caused by that very reason than the young officer had any idea of.

"Thanks, officer. I'll slow down," Raleigh said as he put his identification back in his pocket and waited for the trooper to leave.

"I'm sorry," Valentine whispered.

"Why?" Raleigh joked, hoping she would open up and talk to him now that the tension had been broken. "Did you have your foot over here on the gas and I didn't realize it in my misery?"

Valentine wished he'd said something besides "misery." In her own misery she shook her head, but she had nothing more to say. She just wanted to go home and sort out her thoughts—if that was even possible.

What she really wanted to do, she told herself honestly, was crawl into her bed, pull the covers over her head, and weep like a young child. After all her warnings to herself, she'd still made a fool of herself with Raleigh. And now it was beginning to hurt like hell.

Valentine wasn't sure how long it took them to get back to her house, but she did know that she'd never

seen such a welcome sight in her life. The moment Raleigh stopped the car, she bolted from it. She was inside
with her door locked before he even had time to come
around to her side of the car.

She leaned against the door, breathing harshly, until
she heard Raleigh start the car. It seemed like forever
before he left, but when he finally pulled away, she
stripped off her clothes as she walked, not caring where
they fell.

Then she climbed into her bed, curled up in the fetal
position, and sobbed as she hadn't since she was accused of embezzling from the bank. She'd never
thought she could hurt that badly again, but now, she
hurt worse.

She hurt so far down inside herself that she was sure
the wound would never heal this time. It was a place
Raleigh had touched intimately with a very personal part
of himself and she could never change that, never wipe
away either the feeling or the memory. Of that she was
sure.

Raleigh couldn't face going back to Tod and Carolyn's tonight. He wanted to be alone. He needed time to
think. He decided he might as well go all the way back
to the lake. Anyway, someone had to clean up the birthday food. He didn't want to find a bunch of ants feast-
ing there the next time he went.

When he returned to the living room, he struck a
match to see where he was walking. The blanket and
food lay where they had left them. Raleigh lit the candles again, but nothing was the same now. The cottage
was empty and cold. The only evidence that anyone had

been there at all was the mussed side of the blanket where he and Valentine had made love.

He stared at the cake for a moment; then, in a sudden fit of rage, he took the ends of the blanket and tumbled everything toward the middle—cake, expensive china, food, and wine. Then he tied the four ends of the blanket together and tossed it out on the porch.

Tomorrow he would throw the whole thing away. He didn't want to be reminded of how wrong tonight had gone. He walked down to the water's edge and stared at the black water as it lapped the surrounding shore, and he wished he could find some answers there.

How Valentine got up and went to work the next morning as though it were any other morning in her life, she never knew. She mechanically set about the business of baking, trying her very best to concentrate on nothing but her work, yet each time she moved, her body reminded her of the exquisite love she'd shared with Raleigh. She was still alive with sensations and memories. The night had done nothing to ease that or the heartache.

When Lucy came in, she was all sunshine and eagerness. "What did Mr. Coseegan think of his birthday cake?" she asked enthusiastically.

Valentine swallowed. Ah, the birthday cake they had left untouched on that gorgeous blanket with the supper wasting on the elegant china. The blanket where they had made love in such a frenzy of thrills and passion.

"Valentine?" Lucy prompted. "Didn't he like it? Didn't he have a sense of humor?"

Valentine forced herself to smile. "He thought it was

cute, but naturally he jokingly took exception to being called over the hill."

Lucy chuckled heartily. "I'm sure no one has ever called that man over the hill before. I declare, Miss Smith, he's the most handsome man I think I've ever seen. I just know he drives the ladies wild." She winked at her boss. "He wouldn't be a bad catch for you, missy, and you know I've been telling you it's time you saw gentlemen friends."

She reached out and patted Valentine on the shoulder. "I'll tell you something else. I think he likes you. I'll bet if you just gave him the slightest bit of encouragement, he'd ask you out by himself instead of with his sister and brother-in-law. By the way, how did the birthday party go, and what did he do with the rest of the cake?"

Valentine tried to keep the smile on her face. "It wasn't much of a party," she said, not wanting to go into any of it. "We even decided to keep the cake and share it with the wedding guests since I'd made such a large one and so much was left."

They hadn't even cut it, she thought unhappily. She wondered what Raleigh had done with it.

"That's a fine idea," Lucy said, interrupting Valentine's thoughts.

Lucy clasped her hands together and looked angelic. "I just love weddings. I'm so thrilled about this one. It's so exciting to have the town participate in something like this. You know, when I was a girl, they held festivals at the park. There was music and dancing and fun. I think this wedding will be like that—a fun time for absolutely everyone who comes. Don't you think so?"

Valentine managed to nod, then she glanced up when the bell rang. A customer was coming in, thank God. Her relief turned to panic when she saw dark blond hair and thought the man was Raleigh. But her mind was just playing tricks on her. She wasn't sure if she was disappointed or glad.

Raleigh hadn't made any decisions or changes in plans, despite spending most of the night sitting on the deck, staring at the water. Well, that wasn't quite the truth, he told himself.

He was going to visit old Mr. Carruthers this morning and buy the building that housed Valentine's shop. If all went well, he would give it to her as a wedding present when he returned from his assignment.

If no wedding ever took place, the building would still be hers. She would not be at the mercy of any man, especially an old geezer like Mr. Carruthers.

Raleigh had asked Carolyn and Tod about the old man and discovered that this kind of tactic wasn't unusual for him. He had a penchant for pretty young women, and Valentine was pretty, no doubt about that.

Raleigh smiled. There was no doubt about that at all, and he couldn't fault the old man for thinking so. It was the pressure he placed on Valentine that set Raleigh off.

Valentine. Through the long hours of the night, he had remembered how his body had felt against hers, how warm and receptive she had been to his kisses and caresses, how responsive to his loving.

"Hell!" he muttered aloud. If he let himself keep thinking about that, he'd go crazy for sure. All he wanted to do this morning was go to the shop and try all over again to explain his position, but he'd discovered last night that was useless and pointless.

Instead, he would take his frustrations out on old Mr. Carruthers. He'd already made the preliminary call about discussing the possible purchase of the building, explaining who he was and why he wanted that particular building. Mr. Carruthers, the sly old fox, hadn't hesitated in conversation at all when Raleigh had said he wanted the entire building for a wedding gift for his future bride, Valentine Smith.

"Fine girl. Fine girl," the old man said, then proceeded to talk about how valuable the property was on Main Street.

Raleigh smiled again. He was way ahead of Carruthers. He'd investigated prices the moment the real estate offices opened, and he'd been able to speak knowledgeably about both price and potential in the area.

He had no doubt in the world that he would get the building—and at a reasonable price. He just wondered what Valentine would think about the purchase.

CHAPTER TEN

DAYS PASSED AND Valentine tried her best to keep busy with the wedding arrangements, which should have been easy enough to do, but she couldn't stop thinking about Raleigh. She was surprised when he called her one afternoon, acting as though nothing in the world had happened between them. Her palms were sweating, her heart was pounding, and she didn't think she could talk at all.

"I have that extra key to the cottage," Raleigh said. "Since the wedding is next week, I desperately need you to help me decorate. I know how busy you are, but can you find any time at all just to ride out and help me decide on colors for carpet and blinds?"

"I—I—" Valentine licked her lips. She didn't know what to say. How could he talk to her so easily, so casually?

She stiffened her spine. She wouldn't let him know again how badly he had hurt her. She had walked into it with her eyes wide open, just as she had agreed to do the wedding and to help him decorate the wedding cottage. If he could go blandly about business, she would do her best to pretend she could too.

"Yes, I think I can find a couple of hours, this afternoon, in fact," she said, over the wild beating of her heart. She truly didn't know if she could even look at him again. His very voice sent her senses spinning.

"Fine. Shall I pick you up there at five?"

She almost said five-fifteen, so she could have time to freshen up. But what was the point?

"Fine." Then she hung up. She couldn't have said another word if she had to. She thought she might cry or faint as it was, and she didn't know which would make her feel better.

"Who was that?" Lucy asked.

"Raleigh Coseegan."

"Oh, is he checking on the wedding preparations?" Lucy asked, smiling.

Valentine found a smile from somewhere and pasted it on her lips. "It's a secret, as you know, Lucy, but he's giving Randolph and Mimmi a cottage at Smith Mountain Lake. I helped him pick it out, and I'm going to help him decorate it a bit. Just some colors and that kind of thing. He's running out of time, so I'll ride out with him this evening after work."

She could see the twinkle in Lucy's eyes. "I see." The older woman clasped her hands together and winked. "I told you he's interested in you, Miss Smith.

Why I wouldn't be surprised if another wedding came about from all of this."

"Lucy, you're such a romantic," Valentine scoffed more bitterly than she had intended. "The man's a womanizer. He's not interested in getting married, believe me."

Lucy frowned, remembering the first conversation she'd had with Raleigh Coseegan. He really hadn't sounded very interested in marriage. Still, if she was any judge of things— She shrugged. What did she know. An old fool like her? Maybe she *was* too romantic. Still, it seemed such a shame. She thought the young couple would be perfect together.

When Raleigh came to pick her up that evening, Valentine was a nervous wreck. She didn't know why she hadn't had the nerve to tell him she simply didn't have time to help him with the decorating. She supposed it was that old loyalty fixation she had.

Damn! she thought to herself. It was no such thing, and she well knew it. She wanted to see Raleigh so badly she ached with it. She wanted *him* so badly she ached with it. Foolish, stupid woman that she was! She was already regretting the fact that he was seeing her all frazzled from a long day at work.

"Hi!" Raleigh said, just as casually as ever. He was amazed that he could speak at all. Just seeing the woman again haunted him. What on earth was going to become of the two of them? Was there any hope?

"Hello," Valentine said quietly.

She could hardly look him in the eyes. Didn't he know what he did to her? Surely after what they'd shared he felt *something* for her besides social friendliness! Or was she the only fool who thought such things as making love to someone meant something? Wasn't that just like a woman? Apparently Lucy wasn't the only romantic. And Valentine knew better than to be a love-struck fool!

"Ready?" Raleigh asked.

Valentine sighed. She was as ready as she'd ever be. Without a word, she followed him out the door, locked it behind her, and inhaled deeply, hoping it would calm her a little.

"How's the wedding baking going?" Raleigh asked cheerfully.

He was surprised by the sound of his own voice, but, oddly, once Valentine was in the car with him, he began to feel more hopeful. He wasn't exactly sure what he was hopeful about, but his spirits were lifted all the same. He didn't know what he would have done if she'd refused to see him again.

"Oh, fine," she said, pleased to be on a subject almost as dear to her heart as Raleigh. "Everyone is working so well together." Her eyes sparkled as she looked at him. "Raleigh, I never knew anything could be such fun. It's put the whole town in a good mood—well, all but the grouchiest of them, at least."

Raleigh instantly thought of Carruthers. "How's that landlord of yours? What's he think of the wedding?"

Valentine frowned. "To tell you the truth, I really don't know. He hasn't come around at all this week."

"I gather that's unusual." Raleigh concluded innocently.

"Unusual?" she repeated, a trace of bitterness evident

before she quickly caught herself. "Yes, he can be a bit of a pest when he wants to be."

Raleigh winked at her. "I can't say that I blame him. You're the kind of woman who causes a man to make a pest of himself."

Valentine quickly looked out the window. She didn't know what to say. She was growing uncomfortable again.

Raleigh sighed raggedly. He loved this woman. And what now?

"I believe Mimmi's parents have arrived, haven't they?" Valentine asked, clutching at the first subject that came to mind.

Raleigh nodded. "Yes. They're absolutely charming, and so thrilled about the wedding."

"Do they speak English?" Valentine asked, looking at Raleigh. Her breath caught in her throat. She was so drawn to him. Even now, after all that had happened, all she wanted to do was pull him into her arms and make love to him.

He chuckled. "About four words: 'Thank you,' 'toilet,' 'eat,' and 'good-bye.'"

Valentine laughed softly. "They sound like pretty good words to know."

Both of them laughed, and Raleigh resisted the urge to reach over and clasp her hand in his. "This wedding's going to be a lot of fun," he said, "and you're responsible for much of that."

"I can hardly take sole credit," she demurred. "Everyone has pulled together so beautifully. In fact, I think we'll have more food than we can use. You could have ordered half of what I'm baking and still have food left over. Everyone seems to want to bring something to eat."

Raleigh grinned at her. "Ah, that's true, but no one has the talent you have. Everything else will go untouched until your goodies are all gone."

"Thanks," she said, flattered. She was always so easily flattered by this man, she reminded herself.

She was nervous all over again when they reached the cottage, but fortunately Raleigh made the experience easy, and they ended up staying quite some time. The electricity had been turned on, and at last they decided on colors, carpet, and wallpaper from the samples Raleigh had picked up earlier.

Valentine was back home by ten P.M. All the way back, she had wondered if he would try to kiss her, try to talk to her, try to approach her in any way. She shouldn't have worried. To her surprise, he handed her a key to the cottage.

"If you have any free time to take a run out there and check on things, I'd really be grateful. I could do it myself, but I wouldn't know if we were getting what we wanted or not. Honest, I'm hopeless in the house department."

Valentine found it truly hard to believe that this man was hopeless in any department. He was simply too accomplished, too capable, but she didn't protest.

"I'll check as soon as the installers start to work and again before the wedding," she promised. "I agreed, and I won't let you down."

Raleigh's dark eyes met her blue ones. "I never thought you would, Valentine Smith. Not from the first time I saw you."

She managed a smile. He'd never figured out the first time he saw her—that wretched girl doing that comedic belly dance. At some point she was sure she would look back at that experience and think it was funny, just as Tricia had said, but not right now.

"Thanks," she murmured, turning toward her door.

Raleigh watched until she was inside. "Goodnight," he said.

"Goodnight." Valentine shut the door and once more she was overcome by that empty feeling. Why had she fallen in love with Raleigh Coseegan? Why? Hadn't she had enough heartache in her life already? Even though she promised herself she wouldn't cry, that's exactly what she did. She waited until Raleigh had driven off, but then she walked to her bedroom, lay down, and sobbed.

Storm clouds gathered the day of the wedding. Everyone was in an absolute commotion as it was, and the threat of rain didn't help any. Even though there was a pavilion at the park and plenty of tents had been installed where the food was being set up, no one wanted rain.

The entire park was gloriously decorated. The trees were in natural beautiful bloom and all the tables were bedecked with cherry blossoms and greenery. The nuptials were to take place at two P.M., so the whole ensemble was praying the rain would hold off until evening.

Those people participating in the wedding preparations were bustling about, getting things in order. Valentine and Carolyn both took a moment to stand back and admire the way the proceedings were going. The crowd was large, but orderly.

When Raleigh walked up behind them, Valentine spun around. Beautifully dressed in a blue tux, Raleigh was impossibly handsome and virile.

"You look wonderful," Valentine exclaimed, before she even thought about it.

"Thank you," he said, winking at her. "You look damned good yourself, but then you always do."

She smiled. "Thank you."

God, how she loved his flattery; she *had* taken special pains to look her best today, despite being the "hired help." She had chosen a spring ensemble of soft pink-and-white silk that moved easily with her. She had worn four-inch heels, even knowing that she would be on her feet a long time and walking on soft ground. Her hair was done in a chignon, and she felt especially attractive.

"And the mother of the groom?" Carolyn prompted. "No compliment for me?"

Walking over to her, Raleigh wrapped his arm around her shoulder and gave her a kiss on the lips.

"Don't, Raleigh!" she protested. "You'll ruin my lipstick!"

He grinned at Valentine and shook his head. "Women! Never happy! I guess you don't want one of my kisses either, do you?"

She could feel her face turn red. She yearned for one of his kisses; she could almost taste it.

"No, I don't want my lipstick ruined either," she said coolly.

That tone again, Raleigh told himself. He could hear it in his sleep!

"Well, I'll see if I can locate the father of the groom," he commented, wanting to walk away before he said more than he should.

"He's gone to pick up the bride and her family," Carolyn said. "The wedding takes place in twenty minutes." She looked up at the sky. "Please hold off rain."

Suddenly a big burly man walked up to Raleigh and slapped him on the back. "Raleigh Coseegan, isn't it?" the man asked jovially.

Raleigh laughed loudly. "As if you didn't know, Harris! Damn, man, when I sent the wedding invitation, I didn't really want you to come," he joked. "I had no idea you'd show up. Weren't you out of the country or something?"

Harris laughed. "I was right up the road in Washington, D.C.; and frankly, my man, the note you included in the wedding invitation made me nervous. I decided I'd better come here and talk some sense into you."

"Save it," Raleigh said a little firmly. "Tom Harris, I want you to meet my sister, Carolyn Duncan, and this is Valentine Smith."

Tom raised his brows. "Charmed, I'm sure, ladies." He gazed openly at Valentine. "No wonder ol' Raleigh here has lost his perspective."

"Harris—" Raleigh warned.

The crowd unexpectedly broke into applause and Valentine, Carolyn, Raleigh, and Tom Harris turned to see Randolph and his best man walking toward the altar that had been set up in the pavilion. A buzz of excitement went through the crowd as they began to head toward the round structure.

"Doesn't my boy look handsome?" Carolyn asked as she started walking along with the others.

"He really does," Valentine agreed.

Another murmur roused the crowd as the bride stepped out of Tod's car. "Oh, she's lovely!" Valentine breathed. "Simply lovely."

"Yes," they all agreed.

The bride had eyes for nobody but the groom as she walked across the grass, two of her bridesmaids holding up the long white train of her gown. Valentine couldn't help but think this wedding was extraordinarily romantic and beautiful. It was like a fairy tale, truly it was.

The crowd was hushed as the vows were exchanged, but when the bride and groom were pronounced man and wife, a roar went up that could be heard everywhere. Then the party really began.

Valentine, Lucy, and Carolyn were amazed at how well it all went. There was plenty of food and drink, and the women's groups eagerly helped serve. A live band provided music to dance to, with Italian and southern customs mingled as Carolyn and her family had wanted. It was an event to be remembered.

All too soon, it was over. The bride held her bouquet high in the air and tossed it. To Valentine's surprise, it landed right in her hands. She hadn't even been trying to catch it. Everyone laughed and she blushed as people made jokes.

Standing off to the side, trying his best to ignore Tom

Harris's coaxing that he not resign, Raleigh watched Valentine catch the bouquet.

"That clinches it," he said suddenly, as if watching her catch the bridal bouquet was all the sign he needed. "I'm marrying that woman and settling down here, Tom, so don't keep levying the pressure."

Tom tugged Raleigh by the arm to a table away from the crowd. "Come on, Raleigh," he said. "What's different about this one? You're not the marrying kind, man. Where did you meet her? What do you know about her? You've only been in town for a few short weeks, for God's sake."

Raleigh laughed. "You won't believe how I met her, Tom," he said. "You see, Randolph wanted a harem of belly dancers for his bachelor party, and there were few to be found in this town, I can tell you." He lowered his voice and began to tell the tale of Angelina and Farrah and what a riot it was.

He was so engrossed in his story that he never saw Valentine and Carolyn walk up to the table where the top layer of the wedding cake had been set aside to be frozen for the bride and groom. For just a moment, Carolyn stared at Valentine as they listened to Raleigh's story.

Valentine couldn't move. She was frozen where she stood. She had been his joke after all, in more ways than one. Shocked, she listened as though she were physically chained to the spot where she stood. She heard him say that she was really a bakery shop owner and that he had bought the building she leased and planned to give it to her.

That was the final straw! It was all Valentine could

take. She didn't want to hear any more. Why had he bothered to buy the building? Did he feel sorry for her, or was it payment for being his diversion while he was in town?

As if on cue, the heavens suddenly opened up and rain began to pour. Everyone started to scatter, giving Valentine just the excuse she needed to flee herself, even though she should have stayed to help clean up. Tears flooded her eyes, mingling with the rain, which was drenching her as she ran toward her car. Her high white heels sank into the ground with each step.

"Valentine, wait!" Carolyn cried, but Valentine wouldn't have stopped for anything in the world. She had no idea where she was going, but she started her car and raced away before anyone could get in front of her and delay her progress.

God, how she hurt deep inside! She really didn't know if she would ever get over this. She did know that she would never love again. She would never treat her heart so carelessly, so recklessly. Once had been bad enough. Twice was a tragedy.

Strangely enough, she realized that it no longer mattered to her what the town thought of her. She had proven herself here. She wasn't worried about her reputation. It didn't even matter, she realized. What mattered was the deep, deep ache she felt in her heart.

Before she even knew where she'd gone, she'd arrived at the cottage she'd helped Raleigh pick out. With a shock, she reminded herself that she had no business here now, even though the honeymoon couple wouldn't take possession for two weeks. They were off to the Bahamas. Yesterday Raleigh had brought them out to show them the house he purchased for them.

For a few minutes Valentine sat in her car, crying; then she climbed out and walked up the drive to the cottage. Her dream cottage. A cottage she had once pretended that Raleigh might have purchased for her. For her and him, she amended. What a joke that was!

Using the key she still had, Valentine couldn't resist walking into the cottage a final time. The cottage where she and Raleigh had made love. The cottage where she had dreamed impossible dreams. She stepped inside and flipped on the lights to offset the gloom and rain of the evening. Then she lovingly went from room to room, recalling how much she'd loved this house the day she saw it. She still loved it; it was decorated beautifully, complete with wicker furniture in several rooms.

She lingered a little longer, then locked the door behind her and went out on the deck to stare at the lake. Impulsively, she tossed her key into the water. It quickly sank out of sight, just like her dreams.

Suddenly lights flashed as someone came up the drive. Oh, good Lord, Valentine thought to herself, what if Randolph and Mimmi had come here before going away! But that couldn't be! They'd had to rush to catch a plane. Unless they'd missed it—

She didn't know what to do. She'd thrown away her key, so she stepped down off the deck and worked her way around the side of the house to the driveway, where she'd parked her car. The rain was still pouring, and she was soaked to the skin when she saw Raleigh get out of his car.

"Valentine!" he cried, running over to her and grasping her shoulders. "God, I hoped you'd be here. When Carolyn told me—"

"Don't touch me, Raleigh Coseegan!" she ordered, her voice cold and trembling. She felt like she was shaking to pieces on the inside.

"Valentine, you're going to listen to me this time. What you heard isn't what you think."

"Oh no?" she asked bitterly. "I didn't hear you say that you've known all along I was your little joke, your little distraction, Angelina, the comedic belly dancer?"

"Yes," he said simply, "you heard me say all that."

"And that you bought the shop for me? Thanks, but no thanks," she said bitterly. "One night of love won't cost you that much."

"Stop it!" he said harshly, shaking her furiously. "You make me so damned angry, putting a price tag on everything! You can't believe that's why I bought the shop."

"Just what—"

"Come inside and listen to me," he said savagely. "I'm tired of all this fooling around and game playing. I despise it, and I don't think we deserve to hurt ourselves this way."

Valentine tried to free herself of his grip, but he was too strong. Thoroughly drenched, both of them went into the shelter of the cottage.

Raleigh flipped the lights back on and faced Valentine, his hands still gripping hers as if he might break them should she try to get away again.

"I tried to tell you the night we made love right here in this cottage," he said sharply, "that I love you, that things weren't the way they seemed, but you, little hard-head, wouldn't listen, and I was too afraid of driving you away."

He freed her abruptly and ran a hand through his wet hair. "I was afraid of myself, too. I was afraid I couldn't go on just one more assignment and settle down here. I promised myself that last time, and yet I took another assignment, but then I met you."

He laughed. "That's why Tom Harris showed up at the wedding. He saw through the letter I wrote, even when I myself thought I was still in doubt. Oh, Valentine," he said with a groan, "when I saw you catch that bouquet, I knew—I *knew*—that I have to spend my lifetime with you—that I need to—want to, whatever you need to label it."

"You knew I was Angelina, the belly dancer, all along, and you didn't tell me," she murmured. "Why?" She was truly afraid to hear his answer.

"I've told you from the start I've wanted you from the first time I saw you. That was the first time, but you were so obviously afraid that someone would find out the dancer was you, I didn't want to scare you off by admitting I knew. I put it all together when I saw you in the bakery and Lucy told me about Carruthers raising the rent to put pressure on you to see him. I didn't want to make any mistakes."

"Raleigh, you wouldn't lie about something like this, would you?" Valentine asked tremulously. She loved him so much it hurt. If he was making a fool of her again, she thought for sure she would just die.

"I fibbed to you only a tiny bit, Valentine," he said, "when I wanted you all to myself that night we made love in this cabin. I didn't want Carolyn and Tod here. I bought this cabin with the idea of eventually living here with you. That's why it was so important that you decorate it, that you love it."

Valentine was stunned. "But what about Randolph and Mimmi? They think you've given them this house for their wedding present."

He shook his head. "I gave them the second one. This one is ours. And the shop—I bought that from old man Carruthers for your wedding present, not to insult you."

He ran his hands through his wet hair again. "I was in this dilemma, you see. I do have to take one more last critical assignment, and I was afraid if I did that I would agree to another and another. Now I know that's not true. I want to settle down here with you, Valentine Smith. I want to marry you. I want you to bake me birthday cakes for the rest of my life."

Valentine suddenly remembered the cake they'd left untouched on that beautiful blanket here. "What did you do with that cake, Raleigh? I didn't see it at the wedding."

He grimaced. "I was in such a state of anguish that I threw everything away—blanket, china, cake and all."

"You didn't?"

He nodded. "I did."

She smiled at him. "Well, it doesn't matter. I'll bake all your birthday cakes for the rest of our lives. You go on your assignment, Raleigh Coseegan, but you come back to me."

"Valentine, love, you can bet on it," he said, drawing her into his arms. "God, we're soaked," he murmured as he kissed her wet face. "Let's go try out our shower and get warm."

Valentine smiled. "Only if we can try out the bed afterward. I'm warm already just from being near you."

Raleigh chuckled. "I've been warm since the first time I saw you, lady. I wouldn't miss trying out our bed for all the world. I want to spend every night there with you for the rest of my life. God, I love you."

"And I love you, Raleigh Coseegan."

He kissed her gently, then led her down the hall of their wedding cottage—their own special love nest, where both of them knew their dreams would come true as their love only deepened with time.

213